WATCH AND WARD

Other Works by Henry James
Published by Grove Press

ITALIAN HOURS

LITERARY REVIEWS AND ESSAYS ON AMERICAN,
ENGLISH, AND FRENCH LITERATURE

A LONDON LIFE

THE REVERBERATOR

THE SACRED FOUNT

Watch and Ward

HENRY JAMES

with an Introduction by

LEON EDEL

GROVE PRESS, INC. / NEW YORK

First Black Cat Edition 1979
First Printing 1979
ISBN: 0-394-17097-0
Grove Press ISBN: 0-8021-4270-2
Library of Congress Catalog Card Number: 60-11089

LIBRARY OF CONGRESS CATALOGING IN PUBLICATION DATA

James, Henry, 1843-1916.
Watch and ward.

Reprint of the 1960 ed. published by Grove Press, New York, in series: An Evergreen book.
I. Title.
[PZ3.J234Wat   1979] [PS2116]   813'.4   79-15759
ISBN 0-394-17097-0

Manufactured in the United States of America

Distributed by Random House, Inc., New York

GROVE PRESS, INC., 196 West Houston Street, New York, N.Y. 10014

INTRODUCTION

Watch and Ward was Henry James's first novel, written on his return to America in 1870 after a year's wandering in Europe. He had high hopes for it. There was even a moment when he dreamed it might be "the great American novel," and that it would make a large place for him on the American literary scene—larger than his scattered tales had done. The story was serialised in the *Atlantic Monthly* from August to December 1871, but was not published in book form until seven years later, that is after he had brought out two other novels, *Roderick Hudson* (1875) and *The American* (1877). When he revised *Watch and Ward* in 1878 he explained to his parents: "If I get any fame, my early things will be sure to be rummaged out and as they are there it is best to take hold of them myself and put them in order. So I lately gave great pains to patching up *Watch and Ward*." It was also a way, he added, of "turning an honest penny."

He patched up the text; indeed he revised it so strenuously that one scholar has counted more than eight hundred verbal changes "and persistent refinements of punctuation."* James did not, however, alter the story itself, and between book covers, as in the magazine, it

* B. R. McElderry Jr., "Henry James's Revision of *Watch and Ward*," *Modern Language Notes,* November 1952, pp. 457–461.

remains a strange little tale of a wealthy Bostonian who adopts a twelve-year-old girl under melodramatic circumstances and brings her up in the hope that she will —in an exercise of free choice—marry him when she comes of age. The theme, it must be recognised, was hardly new; in our time André Gide treated it with great sensitivity in *La Symphonie Pastorale* and more recently Vladimir Nabokov has given us a frivolous treatment of it in *Lolita*. This is not to say that *Watch and Ward* is endowed with the conscious sexuality of the recent works. It contains a peculiar sexuality of its own. I refer to the book's persistent erotic imagery and innocent erotic statement which seems to have been set down with bland unconsciousness on the author's part. It is all the more striking because we are today less sensitive to such things in novels (although more alert to them), and it is a little difficult to believe that Henry James, his copy-readers and the staid *Atlantic* editors could have been such delightful innocents. What are we to make, for example, of the thoughts of Nora, entertained by her guardian after he has adopted her? "I may add also," says the narrator, "that, in his desire to order all things well, Roger caught himself wondering whether, at the worst, a little precursory love-making would do any harm. The ground might be gently tickled to receive his own sowing; the petals of the young girl's nature, playfully forced apart, would leave the golden heart of the flower but the more accessible to his own vertical rays." Strange, in a city as addicted to banning books, that this should have passed unnoticed in Boston.

If we blush now it is for the young Henry James, rather than for what he was saying. He was, after all, twenty-eight; and we have always thought him a rather sophisticated cosmopolitan. We blush as well, perhaps, for the proper Bostonians, who seem to have found nothing improper—or rather inept—in such writing. If these Puritanical gentlemen were alive today they would doubtless assert that we have "dirty" Freudian minds, and that this is really all in our own erotic imaginations. Nevertheless the time was to come—it must be recorded —when both William James and that scrupulous guardian of adolescent reading-matter, William Dean Howells, signalled Henry James that he might be a little more cautious and not quite so sexual in certain of his images. It is the utter innocence of this story which, in a way, endears it to us. *Lolita*, for all its verbal delicacies, is written in full awareness of its theme. *Watch and Ward* is naïve from beginning to end. There are moments when it might have come from the pen of a more amateurish Jane Austen, if not from that of the author of *The Young Visiters*. Indeed, what could be more naïve than the episode of the watch-keys, and we must once more ask ourselves (with our own active Freudian imaginations ticking away furiously) how the future author of *The Wings of the Dove* could allow himself a scene which D. H. Lawrence might have written. Roger and his cousin, the clergyman Hubert, are discussing the adopted girl. They will both be rivals for the girl's affection. Nora has been sent off to bed, but she comes back, announcing that her watch-key has disappeared. She asks her guardian, Roger, for his, and we glimpse her in slight disarray, in "a merino dressing-gown of sombre blue. Her hair was gathered for the night into a single massive coil, which had been loosened by the rapidity of her flight along the passage." Then, as she tries to wind her little watch, Roger's key proves "a complete misfit, so that she had recourse to Hubert's. It hung on the watch-chain which depended from his waistcoat, and some rather intimate fumbling was needed to adjust it to Nora's diminutive timepiece."

We must tell ourselves, of course, that the Victorians were accustomed to winding watches with keys, that they would see no special symbolic significance in this harmless episode. We must tell ourselves also that certain words in our time have taken on sexual overtones which they did not have in James's. Presumably when Roger thinks of "precursory love-making" he is imagining nothing so free and adventurous as the love-making in which Lolita's Humbert Humbert indulges, or the lubricious heroes of our post-war novels. When he uses the word "intimate" he probably means just that and not the intimacy of the bedroom. Nevertheless, the imagery is "suggestive"; it shows us the young James, at his writing-desk, finding verbal release for much libidinal feeling that was later to be artfully disciplined. When he had overcome the awkwardness of his nonage, he could complain that the Anglo-Saxon novel was *too* squeamish, too addicted to tailoring itself for the innocent eyes of adolescent maidens; that it did not allow the writers in the English-speaking world the freedom possessed by their *confrères* across the Channel—that of treating the relationship between men and women in an adult way—"the great relation . . . the constant world-renewal."

II

There is then an undeniable quaintness and a rather old-time charm in *Watch and Ward*: it is sex unconscious of itself, an involuntary account of it in its thick Victorian wrappings. And then the novel has its temporal importance: it occupies, chronologically, the first place on one of the world's famous shelves of fiction. James, however, invariably spoke of *Roderick Hudson* as occupying this place. We can concede the point; we grant that *Watch and Ward* belongs to the period of trial and error, while *Roderick Hudson* marks the emergence of the real Jamesian self. Nevertheless the hard historical fact remains that *Watch and Ward* exists (as Joyce's *Stephen Hero* or Proust's *Jean Santeuil*) and we can hardly dismiss it altogether on the ground that the pen which wrote it surpassed itself later. For one thing the demure tale had its audience: the particular copy which lies before me as I write is clearly marked "Sixth Edition." *Watch and Ward* may have been, as James said after revising it, "very thin and as 'cold' as an icicle," but he also remarked that it would appear "pretty enough." This it seems to have done.*

* James never published the novel in England; its only other publication, after 1878 in Boston, was in the posthumous collective edition of 1921, edited by Percy Lubbock. This has long been out of print.

We read *Watch and Ward,* as we read *Stephen Hero* or *Jean Santeuil,* as the first effort of a novelist destined for greatness, which harbours within it an imagination not yet free, not yet master of itself, not yet fully responsive. If we read it after we have read James's major works, the novel seems like some early sketching out of things to come—a rough telling of *The Portrait of a Lady* or of *Washington Square,* and even, at moments, of the materials out of which James will produce a generation of twinkling American innocents stepping daintily on the cobbles of Europe and somehow getting their rustling dresses spattered with continental mud: as if they should never have left the solid plank sidewalks of Schenectady and the Boston suburbs. And if the book seems to be filled with primordial echoes of later beauty, it has within it as well strange undertones of novels written by other novelists earlier in the century. Nora is the little girl who will replace Silas Marner's gold; Nora, aiding her impecunious cousin George Fenton, is Eugénie Grandet surrendering her small hoard to the glittering Charles. One wonders when James deals with Nora's education whether the novelist may not even be reaching back to *Émile.* Jane Eyre and Rochester are mentioned directly in the text. And the early James cannot resist literary allusion; he fills a whole shelf with volumes read by Nora and her guardian. He also takes time to discourse on the art of fiction:

Is that what they are writing nowadays? [Hubert is speaking to his Nora] I very seldom read a novel, but when I glance into one, I am sure to find some such stuff as that! Nothing irritates me so as the flatness of people's imagination. Common life,—I don't say it's a vision of bliss, but it's better than that. Their stories are like the underside of a carpet,—nothing but the stringy grain of the tissue,—a muddle of figures without shape and flowers without colour. When I read a novel my imagination starts off at a gallop and leaves the narrator hidden in a cloud of dust; I have to come jogging twenty miles back to the dénouement.

The Balzacian image of *L'Envers de l'Histoire Contemporaine* has been translated into the "underside of a carpet," and the future image of the "figure" in that carpet has been forecast.

But for all this, and the narrative awkwardness, the story *moves*; it has a distinct rhythm; the portraits are sketched rapidly and concretely and the observation of American society is often acute. The young writer could tell a story, however much it might be contrived; he could catch the tone of talk; and his early pen has grace and energy. We have only to discover Roger's lavender gloves in the opening sequence to know our man; we have only to listen to Mrs. Keith for a moment or two, to see the future Mrs. Luna as well as the amiable confidantes, those *ficelles* to which James resorted later with so much pleasure. It is particularly rewarding to come upon brief passages, meaningless in this novel, but filled with meaning for the future. We discover, for instance, near the end of the volume, a little detail rich in association for us. Roger is in New York looking for Nora who has run away (horrified at his proposal that she marry him, and feeling not a little that it would be like marrying her father). As he strolls sadly in Central Park he sees two ladies. One.

was of great age and evidently infirm; she came slowly, leaning on her companion's arm; she wore a green shade over her eyes.

She wore a green shade over her eyes. It is a brief descriptive detail. But here, over the eyes of a woman of "great age," James has already placed that object which we will meet again in *The Aspern Papers*. Who, having read the later work, can forget Juliana's everlasting green shade, which hides from the view of the inquisitive narrator those magnificent eyes which once had looked, long, long before, into the eyes of Jeffrey Aspern?

III

The revisions of *Watch and Ward*, unlike the revisions of Henry James's late years, are wholly in the interest of precision and simplicity; they mark the beginning of what was to become an inveterate habit with him—that of subjecting every new edition to a process of close editorial scrutiny. Professor McElderry tells us that in this novel James introduced contractions in the interest of greater variety of speech; he removed bookish words; he eradicated French phrases; he worked the stiffness out of many passages by giving them a conversational rhythm. Thus Roger "annulled his personal share in the business" in the first version, but simply "withdrew altogether from his profession" in the second. There is hardly an instance in which the writer of 1878, standing on the verge of his greatest success (*Daisy Miller* was about to appear), is not the absolute master of his younger self. The touch of the professional supersedes the young and aspiring stylist:

1871	1878
His heart was flattered, rather, by the idea of living at the mercy of that melting impermanence which beguiles us forever with deferred promises.	His heart was flattered, rather, by the idea of living at the mercy of change which might always be change for the better.

or again:

there was something grotesque in his new condition,— in the sudden assumption of paternal care by a man who had seemed to the world to rejoice so placidly in his sleek and comfortable singleness.	there was something comical in a sleek young bachelor turning nurse and governess.

To which we might add, since it is rare in James, the "howler" which escaped the novelist's vigilant pen. In the fifth chapter, when Nora's long talk with Hubert comes to an end, "as she spoke, she caught Hubert's eye in the glass. He dropped it and took up his hat." This belongs with the unconscious humour of the book. For the rest, no one, I think, would quarrel with the revisions, and the text reprinted here is accordingly that of 1878.

13

When he was writing *Watch and Ward*, James boasted to
the editors of the *Atlantic Monthly*, with that swagger he
affected with publishers, that it was "one of the greatest
works of 'this or any age.'" We must recognise that if
this was a Barnum-like boast, it nevertheless reflected the
way in which Henry aspired to greatness. And the fact
that seven years elapsed before he allowed the serial to
become a book testifies to his recognition of its shortcomings. It was conceived as a study of Boston manners,
in the Balzacian mode; read in a biographical light we can
say that it deals rather with the manners of Quincy Street,
the street which harboured the home of the James
family. In the novel we discover, without much difficulty,
Henry James's submerged feelings of this time. We need
not go into the original fantasy—it would take us far
afield; I mean that of the young man who, rejected by the
woman he loves, and playing the lover's role with awkwardness, dreams up a marriage with a wife he will raise
from childhood, one who is almost, by his having
adopted her, a kinswoman. We are to see this situation
dealt with much later in *The Awkward Age*, in the strange
relationship between Mr. Longdon, who had once loved
Nanda's mother, and the adolescent Nanda herself. What
catches our eye, however, is the group of suitors in
Watch and Ward, for they will reappear, with modifi-
cations, in *The Portrait of a Lady* and *The Wings of the
Dove*; and one of them will render Catherine Sloper's
life miserable in *Washington Square*. The "free" young

woman who must "choose"—as Nora does here, and as Isabel does in *The Portrait*—this is the theme enunciated in James's first novel. In the Jamesian world of love and marriage the "heroine of the scene" is invariably surrounded by a particular constellation of aspirants, a little like Portia and the casket-choosers. Thus in "Poor Richard," written four years before *Watch and Ward*, the lover, unlike the traditional hero of romance, is the weakest and least certain of the candidates, prone to illness and always in doubt about his strength and his manhood. He competes usually with a strong figure, generally favoured by the heroine; and there is always another aspirant, who is rather adroit and sometimes even cunning, a manipulator of situations and persons, or sometimes merely a shoddy fortune-hunter. We must beware of making these characters seem simplifications; James is very clever in shuffling them about, combining them, or splitting them into other human units. Sometimes he gives the qualities of one to another. Nevertheless the basic components remain the same. For the sake of convenience let us label the principal suitors in the Jamesian constellation as the Loyal, the Strong and the Cunning. Roger in *Watch and Ward*, and Ralph in *The Portrait of a Lady* are the Loyal; Hubert in the early novel, Caspar in *The Portrait* are the Strong; and the Cunning can take the form of mendacity, as in the case of Fenton, in *Watch and Ward*, or Morris Townsend in *Washington Square*, or become the cruelly brilliant Osmond of *The Portrait*. In these types, and in this grouping, we can see how Henry James translated the fundamental grouping of significant figures in all his childhood and youth. The "mere junior" who felt himself diminished as a boy beside his father and elder brother* was the Loyal one. His "entrenched" father and sometimes his brother, in these distortions of childhood, re-emerged as the Strong; and William could also be cast as the everlasting rival, the Cunning one. It is on some such ground that we can best explain Henry's predilection, even in his adult days, for an analogous series of relationships in certain of his works. They allowed him, it would seem, to give himself, as the loyal, long-suffering hero—in imagination at least—some kind of victory: either an actual marriage, as in *Watch and Ward*, or a moral victory, or sometimes the triumph of resignation and renunciation—even unto death—that is the triumph of being the Dead Mourned Hero.

Hubert Lawrence in *Watch and Ward*, the worldly clergyman, illustrates this process for us. In making him both religious and secular Henry reflects the person of his father who was not of the Church, but a writer on religious subjects. At the same time he endows him with some of William's qualities and describes his relationship to the Loyal hero Roger in these terms:

He and Roger had been much together in early life and had formed an intimacy strangely compounded of harmony and discord. Utterly unlike in temper and tone, they neither thought nor felt, nor acted together on any single point. Roger was constantly differing, mutely and profoundly, and Hubert frankly and sarcastically; but each, nevertheless, seemed to find in the other an irritating counterpart and complement.

* As I have recounted in *Henry James: The Untried Years*.

This is a close picture of Henry's deepest feelings about his elder brother.

That Henry, in writing *Watch and Ward*, was haunted by familial problems may be seen also in his need to compose the principal characters into a family group. Roger and Hubert are cousins; Nora and Fenton are cousins; Nora, adopted by Roger, stands in relation to him as stepdaughter; his role toward her is both paternal and maternal. Only after Hubert is shown to be a vacillating individual, and Fenton a self-seeker, is Roger able to make his stepdaughter his wife. By remaining loyal and devoted he triumphs, but he falls ill, as poor Richard did, or like Ralph (who, however, dies of his illness in *The Portrait*). Like Roger, Ralph all but adopts Isabel Archer, providing her with the fortune that launches her on her adventures in Europe. How far James was to carry this image of himself as the Loyal sufferer, or the dying invalid, we may judge from the transformation of his principal design in *The Wings of the Dove*: here the heroine supplants the hero as invalid; the omnipotence is vested with Sir Luke, the healer; the hero, still weak and unassertive, is manipulated by strong assertive women. The other aspirant is a clumsy and blundering fool.

Today it is possible to say that if *Watch and Ward* is overweighted with the intense personal feelings of the young Henry James, the novelist was still correct in believing that there was something "great" in it. Its themes, after all, were to yield him half a dozen major works. His fault in *Watch and Ward* was that of most first-novelists: he tried to cram all his future performances into the single work; and he achieved a fiction rich in thematic material and overstuffed in performance. Yet it shows us the artist, working within a literary tradition, grasping his form, and in possession of a verbal ear that will give him a transcendent style. As such, *Watch and Ward*, repudiated by its author, disregarded by criticism, is a glimpse, however shadowy, into the creative process of a novelist; and a harbinger of his greatness.

LEON EDEL

New York University

I

ROGER LAWRENCE had come to town for the express purpose of doing a certain act, but as the hour for action approached he felt his ardour rapidly ebbing. Of the ardour that comes from hope, indeed, he had felt little from the first; so little that as he whirled along in the train he wondered to find himself engaged in this fool's errand. But in default of hope he was sustained, I may almost say, by despair. He should fail, he was sure, but he must fail again before he could rest. Meanwhile he was restless enough. In the evening, at his hotel, having roamed aimlessly about the streets for a couple of hours in the dark December cold, he went up to his room and dressed, with a painful sense of having but partly succeeded in giving himself the figure of an impassioned suitor. He was twenty-nine years old, sound and strong, with a tender heart, and a genius, almost, for common-sense; his face told clearly of youth and kindness and sanity, but it had little other beauty. His complexion was so fresh as to be almost absurd in a man of his age,—an effect rather enhanced by a too early baldness. Being extremely short-sighted, he went with his head thrust forward; but as this infirmity is considered by persons who have studied the picturesque to impart an air of distinction, he may have the benefit of the possibility. His figure was compact and sturdy, and, on the whole, his best point; although, owing to an incurable personal shyness, he had a good deal of awkwardness of movement. He was fastidiously neat in his person, and extremely precise and methodical in his habits, which were of the sort supposed to mark a man for bachelorhood. The desire to get the better of his diffidence had given him a certain formalism of manner which many persons found extremely amusing. He was remarkable for the spotlessness of his linen, the high polish of his boots, and the smoothness of his hat. He carried in all weathers a peculiarly neat umbrella. He never smoked; he drank in moderation. His voice, instead of being the robust barytone which his capacious chest led you to expect, was a mild, deferential tenor. He was fond of going early to bed, and was suspected of what is called "fussing" with his health. No one had ever accused him of meanness, yet he passed universally for a cunning economist. In trifling matters, such as the choice of a shoemaker or a dentist, his word carried weight; but no one dreamed of asking his opinion on politics or literature. Here and there, nevertheless, an observer less superficial than the majority would have whispered you that Roger was an undervalued man, and that in the long run he would come out even with the best. "Have you ever studied his face?" such an observer would say. Beneath its simple serenity, over which his ruddy blushes seemed to pass like clouds in a summer sky, there slumbered a fund of exquisite human expression. The eye was excellent; small, perhaps, and somewhat dull, but with a certain appealing depth, like the tender dumbness in the gaze of a dog. In repose Lawrence may have looked stupid; but as he talked his face slowly brightened by gradual fine degrees, until at the end of an hour it inspired you with a confidence so perfect as to be in some degree a tribute to its owner's intellect, as it certainly was to his integrity. On this occasion Roger dressed himself with unusual care and with a certain sober elegance. He debated for three minutes over two cravats, and then, blushing in his mirror at his puerile vanity, he reassumed the plain black tie in which he had travelled. When he had finished dressing it was still too early to go forth on his errand. He went into the reading-room of the hôtel, but here soon appeared two smokers. Wishing not to be infected by their fumes, he crossed over to the great empty drawing-room, sat down, and beguiled his impatience with trying on a pair of lavender gloves.

While he was so engaged there came into the room a person who attracted his attention by the singularity of his conduct. This was a man of less than middle age, good-looking, pale with a pretentious, pointed moustache and various shabby remnants of finery. His face was haggard, his whole aspect was that of grim and hopeless misery. He walked straight to the table in the centre of the room, and poured out and drank without stopping three full glasses of ice-water, as if he were striving to quench some fever in his vitals. He then went to the window, leaned his forehead against the cold pane, and drummed a nervous tattoo with his long stiff finger-nails. Finally he strode over to the fireplace, flung himself into a chair, leaned forward with his head in his hands, and groaned audibly. Lawrence, as he smoothed down his lavender gloves, watched him and reflected. "What an image of fallen prosperity, of degradation and despair! I have been fancying myself in trouble; I have been dejected, doubtful, anxious. I am hopeless. But what is my sentimental sorrow to this?" The unhappy gentleman rose from his chair, turned his back to the chimney-piece, and stood with folded arms gazing at Lawrence, who was seated opposite to him. The young man sustained his glance, but with sensible discomfort. His face was as white as ashes, his eyes were as lurid as coals. Roger had never seen anything so tragic as the two long harsh lines which descended from his nose, beside his mouth, in seeming mockery of his foppish, relaxed moustache. Lawrence felt that his companion was going to address him; he began to draw off his gloves. The stranger suddenly came towards him, stopped a moment, eyed him again with insolent intensity, and then seated himself on the sofa beside him. His first movement was to seize the young man's arm. "He is simply crazy!" thought Lawrence. Roger was now able to appreciate the pathetic disrepair of his appearance. His open waistcoat displayed a soiled and crumpled shirt-bosom, from whose empty buttonholes the studs had recently been wrenched. In his normal freshness he must have looked like a gambler with a run of luck. He spoke in a rapid, excited tone, with a hard petulant voice.

"You'll think me crazy, I suppose. Well, I shall be soon. Will you lend me a hundred dollars?"

"Who are you? What is your trouble?" Roger asked.

"My name would tell you nothing. I'm a stranger here. My trouble,—it's a long story! But it's grievous, I assure you. It's pressing upon me with a fierceness that grows while I sit here talking to you. A hundred dollars would stave it off,—a few days at least. Don't refuse me!" These last words were uttered half as an entreaty, half as a threat. "Don't say you haven't got them,—a man that wears such pretty gloves! Come; you look like a good fellow. Look at me! I'm a good fellow, too. I don't need to swear to my being in distress."

Lawrence was touched, disgusted, and irritated. The man's distress was real enough, but there was something horribly disreputable in his manner. Roger declined to entertain his request without learning more about him. From the stranger's persistent reluctance to do more than simply declare that he was from St. Louis, and repeat that he was in a tight place, in a d———d tight place, Lawrence was led to believe that he had been dabbling in crime. The more he insisted upon some definite statement of his circumstances, the more fierce and peremptory became the other's petition. Lawrence was before all things deliberate and perspicacious; the last man in the world to be hustled and bullied. It was quite out of his nature to do a thing without distinctly knowing why. He of course had no imagination, which, as we know, should always stand at the right hand of charity; but he had good store of that wholesome discretion whose place is at the left. Discretion told him that his companion was a dissolute scoundrel, who had sinned through grievous temptation, perhaps, but who had certainly sinned. His misery was palpable, but Roger felt that he could not patch up his misery without in some degree condoning his vices. It was not in his power, at any rate, to present him, out of hand, a hundred dollars. He compromised. "I can't think of giving you the sum you ask," he said. "I have no time, moreover, to investigate your case at present. If you will meet me here to-morrow morning, I will listen to anything you shall have made up your mind to say. Meanwhile, here are ten dollars."

The man looked at the proffered note and made no movement to accept. Then raising his eyes to Roger's face,—eyes streaming with tears of helpless rage and baffled want,—"O, the devil!" he cried. "What can I do with ten dollars? D———n it, I don't know how to beg. Listen to me! If you don't give me what I ask, I shall cut my throat! Think of that. On your head be the penalty!"

Lawrence pocketed his note and rose to his feet. "No, decidedly," he said, "you don't know how to beg!" A moment after, he had left the hotel and was walking rapidly toward a well-remembered dwelling. He was shocked and discomposed by this brutal collision with want and vice; but as he walked, the cool night air suggested sweeter things. The image of his heated petitioner was speedily replaced by the calmer figure of Isabel Morton.

He had come to know Isabel Morton three years before, through a visit she had then made to one of his neighbours in the country. In spite of his unventurous tastes and the even tenor of his habits, Lawrence was by no means lacking, as regards life, in what the French call *les grandes curiosités*; but from an early age his curiosity had chiefly taken the form of a timid but strenuous desire to fathom the depths of matrimony. He had dreamed of this gentle bondage as other men dream of the "free unhoused condition" of celibacy. He had been born a marrying man, with a conscious desire for progeny. The world in this respect had not done him justice. It had supposed him to be wrapped up in his petty comforts: whereas, in fact, he was serving a devout apprenticeship to the profession of husband and father. Feeling at twenty-six that he had something to offer a woman, he allowed himself to become interested in Miss Morton. It was rather odd that a man of tremors and blushes should in this line have been signally bold; for Miss Morton had the reputation of being extremely fastidious, and was supposed to wear some dozen broken hearts on her girdle, as an Indian wears the scalps of his enemies.

It is said that, as a rule, men fall in love with their opposites; certainly Lawrence's mistress was not fashioned in his own image. He was the most unobtrusively natural of men; she, on the other hand, was pre-eminently artificial. She was pretty, but not really so pretty as she seemed; clever, but not intelligent; amiable, but not sympathetic. She possessed in perfection the manner of society, which she lavished with indiscriminate grace on the just and the unjust, and which very effectively rounded and completed the somewhat meagre outline of her personal character. In reality, Miss Morton was keenly ambitious. A woman of simpler needs, she might very well have accepted our hero. He offered himself with urgent and obstinate warmth. She esteemed him more than any man she had known,—so she told him; but she added that the man she married must satisfy her heart. Her heart, she did not add, was bent upon a carriage and diamonds.

From the point of view of ambition, a match with Roger Lawrence was not worth discussing. He was therefore dismissed with gracious but inexorable firmness. From this moment the young man's sentiment hardened into a passion. Six months later he heard that Miss Morton was preparing to go to Europe. He sought her out before her departure, urged his suit afresh, and lost it a second time. But his passion had cost too much to be flung away unused. During her residence abroad he wrote her three letters, only one of which she briefly answered, in terms which amounted to little more than this: "Dear Mr. Lawrence, *do* leave me alone!" At the end of two years she returned, and was now visiting her married brother. Lawrence had just heard of her arrival, and had come to town to make, as we have said, a supreme appeal.

Her brother and his wife were out for the evening; Roger found her in the drawing-room, under the lamp, teaching a stitch in crochet to her niece, a little girl of ten, who stood leaning at her side. She seemed to him prettier than before; although, in fact, she looked older and stouter. Her prettiness, for the most part, however, was a matter of coquetry; and naturally, as youth departed, coquetry filled the vacancy. She was fair and plump, and she had a very pretty trick of suddenly turning her head and showing a charming white throat and ear. Above her well-filled corsage these objects produced a most agreeable effect. She always dressed in light colours, but with unerring taste. Charming as she may have been, there was, nevertheless, about her so marked a want of the natural, that, to admire her particularly, it was necessary to be, like Roger, in love with her. She received him with such flattering friendliness and so little apparent suspicion of his purpose, that he almost took heart and hope. If she did not fear a declaration, perhaps she desired one. For the first half-hour Roger's attack hung fire. Isabel talked to better purpose than before she went abroad, and for the moment he sat tongue-tied for very modesty. Miss Morton's little niece was a very pretty child; her hair was combed out into a golden cloud, which covered her sloping shoulders. She kept her place beside her aunt, clasping one of the latter's hands, and staring at Lawrence with that sweet curiosity of little girls. There glimmered mistily in the young man's brain a vision of a home-scene in the future,—a lamp-lit parlour on a winter night, a placid wife and mother wreathed in household smiles, a golden-haired child, and, in the midst, his sentient self, drunk with possession and gratitude. As the clock struck nine the little girl was sent to bed, having been kissed by her aunt and rekissed—or unkissed shall I say?—by her aunt's lover. When she had disappeared, Roger proceeded to business. He had proposed so often to Miss Morton, that, actually, practice had begun to tell. It took but a few moments to make his meaning plain. Miss Morton addressed herself to her niece's tapestry, and, as her lover went on with manly eloquence, glanced up at him from her work with feminine keenness. He spoke of his persistent love, of his long waiting and his passionate hope.

27

Her acceptance of his hand was the only thing that could make him happy. He should never love another woman; if she now refused him, it was the end of all things; he should continue to exist, to work and act, to eat and sleep, but he should have ceased to *live*.

"In Heaven's name," he said, "don't answer me as you have answered me before."

She folded her hands, and with a serious smile, "I shall not, altogether," she said. "When I have refused you before, I have simply told you that I could not love you. I cannot love you, Mr. Lawrence! I must repeat it again to-night, but with a better reason than before. I love another man; I am engaged."

Roger rose to his feet like a man who has received a heavy blow and springs forward in self-defence. But he was indefensible, his assailant inattackable. He sat down again and hung his head. Miss Morton came to him and took his hand and demanded of him, as a right, that he should be resigned. "Beyond a certain point," she said, "you have no right to thrust your regrets upon me. The injury I do you in refusing you is less than that I should do you in accepting you without love."

He looked at her with his eyes full of tears. "Well! I shall never marry," he said. "There is something you cannot refuse me. Though I shall never possess you, I may at least espouse your memory and live in intimate union with your image. I shall live with my eyes fixed upon it." She smiled at this fine talk; she had heard so much in her day! He had fancied himself prepared for the worst, but as he walked back to his hotel, it seemed intolerably bitter. Its bitterness, however, quickened his temper, and prompted a violent reaction. He would now, he declared, cast his lot with pure reason. He had tried love and faith, but they would none of him. He had made a woman a goddess, and she had made him a fool. He would henceforth care neither for woman nor man, but simply for comfort, and, if need should be, for pleasure. Beneath this gathered gust of cynicism the future lay as hard and narrow as the silent street before him. He was absurdly unconscious that good humour was lurking round the very next corner.

It was not till near morning that he was able to sleep. His sleep, however, had lasted less than an hour when it was interrupted by a loud noise from the adjoining room. He started up in bed, lending his ear to the stillness. The sound was immediately repeated; it was that of a pistol-shot. This second report was followed by a loud, shrill cry. Roger jumped out of bed, thrust himself into his trousers, quitted his room, and ran to the neighbouring door. It opened without difficulty, and revealed an astonishing scene. In the middle of the floor lay a man, in his trousers and shirt, his head bathed in blood, his hand grasping the pistol from which he had just sent a bullet through his brain. Beside him stood a little girl in her nightdress, her long hair on her shoulders, shrieking and wringing her hands. Stooping over the prostrate body, Roger recognised, in spite of his bedabbled visage, the person who had addressed him in the parlour of the hotel. He had kept the spirit, if not the letter, of his menace. "O father, father, father!" sobbed the little girl. Roger, overcome with horror and pity, stooped towards her and opened his arms. She, conscious of nothing but the presence of human help, rushed into his embrace and buried her head in his grasp.

The rest of the house was immediately aroused, and the room invaded by a body of lodgers and servants. Soon followed a couple of policemen, and finally the proprietor in person. The fact of suicide was so apparent that Roger's presence was easily explained. From the child nothing but sobs could be obtained. After a vast amount of talking and pushing and staring, after a physician had affirmed that the stranger was dead, and the ladies had passed the child from hand to hand through a bewildering circle of caresses and questions, the multitude dispersed, and the little girl was borne away in triumph by the proprietor's wife, further investigation being appointed for the morrow. For Roger, seemingly, this was to have been a night of sensations. There came to him, as it wore away, a cruel sense of his own accidental part in his neighbour's tragedy. His refusal to help the poor man had brought on the catastrophe. The idea haunted him awhile; but at last, with an effort, he dismissed it. The next man, he assured himself, would have done no more than he; might possibly have done less. He felt, however, a certain indefeasible fellowship in the sorrow of the little girl. He lost no time, the next morning, in calling on the wife of the proprietor. She was a kindly woman enough, but so thoroughly the mistress of a public house that she seemed to deal out her very pity over a bar. She exhibited toward her protégée a hard, business-like charity which foreshadowed vividly to Roger's mind the poor child's probable portion in life, and repeated to him the little creature's story, as she had been able to learn it. The father had come in early in the evening, in great trouble and excitement, and had made her go to bed. He had kissed her and cried over her and, of course, made her cry. Late at night she was aroused by feeling him again at her bedside, kissing her, fondling her, raving over her. He bade her good-night and passed into the adjoining room, where she heard him fiercely knocking about. She was very much frightened; she fancied he was out of his mind. She knew that their troubles had lately been thickening fast; now the worst had come. Suddenly he called her. She asked what he wanted, and he bade her get out of bed and come to him. She trembled, but she obeyed. On reaching the threshold of his room she saw the gas turned low, and her father standing in his shirt against the door at the other end. He ordered her to stop where she was. Suddenly she heard a loud report and felt beside her cheek the wind of a bullet. He had aimed at her with a pistol. She retreated in terror to her own bedside and buried her head in the clothes. This, however, did not prevent her from hearing a second report, followed by a deep groan. Venturing back again, she found her father on the floor, bleeding from the face. "He meant to kill her, of course," said the landlady, "that she mightn't be left alone in the world. It's a wonderful mixture of cruelty and kindness!"

It seemed to Roger an altogether pitiful tale. He related his own interview with the deceased, and the latter's

31

menace of suicide. "It gives me," he said, "a sickening sense of connection with this bloodshed. But how could I help it? All the same, I wish he had taken my ten dollars."

Of the antecedent history of the dead man they could learn little. The child had recognised Lawrence, and had broken out again into a quivering convulsion of tears. Little by little, from among her sobs, they gathered a few facts. Her father had brought her during the preceding month from St. Louis; they had stopped some time in New York. Her father had been for months in great want of money. They had once had money enough; she could not say what had become of it. Her mother had died many months before; she had no other kindred nor friends. Her father may have had friends, but she never saw them. She could indicate no source of possible assistance or sympathy. Roger put the poor little fragments of her story together. The most salient fact among them all was her absolute destitution.

"Well, sir," said the proprietress, "living customers are better than dead ones; I must go about my business. Perhaps you can learn something more." The little girl sat on the sofa with a pale face and swollen eyes, and, with a stupefied, helpless stare, watched her friend depart. She was by no means a pretty child. Her clear auburn hair was thrust carelessly into a net with broken meshes, and her limbs encased in a suit of rusty, scanty mourning. In her appearance, in spite of her childish innocence and grief, there was something undeniably vulgar. "She looks as if she belonged to a circus troupe," Roger said to himself. Her face, however, though without beauty, was not without interest. Her forehead was symmetrical and her mouth expressive. Her eyes were light in colour, yet by no means colourless. A sort of arrested, concentrated brightness, a soft introversion of their rays, gave them a remarkable depth. "Poor little betrayed, unfriended mortal!" thought the young man.

"What is your name?" he asked.

"Nora Lambert," said the child.

"How old are you?"

"Twelve."

"And you live in St. Louis?"

"We used to live there. I was born there."

"Why had your father come to the East?"

"To make money."

"Where was he going to live?"

"Anywhere he could find business."

"What was his business?"

"He had none. He wanted to find some."

"You have no friends nor relations?"

The child gazed a few moments in silence. "He told me when he woke me up and kissed me, last night, that I had not a friend in the world nor a person that cared for me."

Before the exquisite sadness of this statement Lawrence was silent. He leaned back in his chair and looked at the child,—the little forlorn, precocious, potential woman. His own sense of recent bereavement rose powerful in his heart and seemed to respond to hers. "Nora," he said, "come here."

She stared a moment, without moving, and then left

the sofa and came slowly towards him. She was tall for her years. She laid her hand on the arm of his chair and he took it. "You have seen me before," he said. She nodded. "Do you remember my taking you last night in my arms?" It was his fancy that, for an answer, she faintly blushed. He laid his hand on her head and smoothed away her thick disordered hair. She submitted to his consoling touch with a plaintive docility. He put his arm round her waist. An irresistible sense of her childish sweetness, of her tender feminine promise, stole softly into his pulses. A dozen caressing questions rose to his lips. Had she been to school? Could she read and write? Was she musical? She murmured her answers with gathering confidence. She had never been to school; but her mother had taught her to read and write a little, and to play a little. She said almost with a smile, that she was very backward. Lawrence felt the tears rising to his eyes; he felt in his heart the tumult of a new emotion. Was it the inexpugnable instinct of paternity? Was it the restless ghost of his buried hope? He thought of his angry vow the night before to live only for himself and turn the key on his heart. "From the lips of babes and sucklings . . ."—he softly mused. Before twenty-four hours had elapsed a child's fingers were fumbling with the key. He felt deliciously contradicted; he was after all but a lame egotist. Was he to believe, then, that he could not live without love, and that he must take it where he found it? His promise to Miss Morton seemed still to vibrate in his heart. But there was love and love! He could be a protector, a father, a brother. What was the child before him but a tragic embodiment of the misery of isolation, a warning from his own blank future? "God forbid!" he cried. And as he did so, he drew her towards him and kissed her.

At this moment the landlord appeared with a scrap of paper, which he had found in the room of the deceased; it being the only object which gave a clue to his circumstances. He had evidently burned a mass of papers just before his death, as the grate was filled with fresh ashes. Roger read the note, which was scrawled in a hurried, vehement hand, and ran as follows:—

"This is to say that I must—I must—I must! Starving without a friend in the world, and a reputation worse than worthless,—what can I do? Life's impossible. Try it yourself. As regards my daughter,—anything, everything is cruel; but this is the shortest way."

"She has had to take the longest, after all," said the proprietor, *sotto voce*, with a kindly wink at Roger. The landlady soon reappeared with one of the ladies who had been present overnight,—a little pushing, patronising woman, who seemed strangely familiar with the various devices of applied charity. "I have come to arrange," she said, "about our subscription for the little one. I shall not be able to contribute myself, but I will go round among the other ladies with a paper. I have just been seeing the reporter of the *Universe*; he is to insert a kind of 'appeal,' you know, in his account of the affair. Perhaps this gentleman will draw up our paper? And I think it will be a beautiful idea to take the child with me."

Lawrence was sickened. The world's tenderness had fairly begun. Nora gazed at her energetic benefactress, and then, with her eyes, appealed mutely to Roger. Her glance, somehow, moved him to the soul. Poor little disfathered daughter,—poor little uprooted germ of womanhood! Her innocent eyes seemed to more than beseech,—to admonish almost, and command. Should he speak and rescue her? Should he subscribe the whole sum, in the name of human charity? He thought of the risk. She was an unknown quantity. Her nature, her heritage, her good and bad possibilities, were an unsolved problem. Her father had been an adventurer; what had her mother been? Conjecture was useless; she was a vague spot of light on a dark background. He was unable even to decide whether, after all, she was plain.

"If you want to take her round with you," said the landlady to her companion, "I had better just sponge off her face."

"No indeed!" cried the other, "she is much better as she is. If I could only have her little nightgown with the blood on it! Are you sure the bullet didn't strike your dress, deary? I am sure we can easily get fifty names at five dollars apiece. Two hundred and fifty dollars. Perhaps this gentleman will make it three hundred. Come, sir, now!"

Thus adjured, Roger turned to the child. "Nora," he said, "you know you are quite alone. You have no home." Her lips trembled, but her eyes were fixed and fascinated. "Do you think you could love me?" She flushed to the tender roots of her tumbled hair. "Will you come and try?" Her range of expression of course was limited; she could only answer by another burst of tears.

II

"I HAVE adopted a little girl, you know," Roger said, after this, to a number of his friends; but he felt, rather, as if she had adopted him. He found it somewhat difficult to make his terms with the sense of actual paternity. It was indeed an immense satisfaction to feel, as time went on, that there was small danger of his repenting of his bargain. It seemed to him more and more that he had obeyed a divine voice; though indeed he was equally conscious that there was something comical in a sleek young bachelor turning nurse and governess. But for all this he found himself able to look the world squarely in the face. At first it had been with an effort, a blush, and a deprecating smile that he spoke of his pious venture; but very soon he began to take a robust satisfaction in alluding to it freely. There was but one man of whose jocular verdict he thought with some annoyance,—his cousin Hubert Lawrence, namely, who was so terribly clever and trenchant, and who had been through life a commentator formidable to his modesty, though, in the end, always absolved by his good nature. But he made up his mind that, though Hubert might laugh, he himself was serious; and to prove it equally to himself and his friends, he determined on a great move. He withdrew altogether from his profession, and prepared to occupy his house in the country. The latter was immediately transformed into a home for Nora,—a home admirably fitted to become the starting-point of a happy life. Roger's dwelling stood in the midst of certain paternal acres,—a little less than a "place," a little more than a farm; deep in the country, and yet at two hours' journey from town. Of recent years a dusty disorder had fallen upon the house, telling of its master's long absences and his rare and restless visits. It was but half lived in. But beneath this pulverous deposit the rigid household gods of a former generation stand erect on their pedestals. As Nora grew older, she came to love her new home with an almost passionate fondness, and to cherish its transmitted memories as a kind of compensation for her own obliterated past. There had lived with Lawrence for many years an elderly woman, of exemplary virtue, Lucinda Brown by name, who had been a personal attendant of his mother, and since her death had remained in his service as the lonely warden of his villa. Roger had an old-time regard for her, and it seemed to him that her housewifely gossip might communicate to little Nora a ray of his mother's peaceful domestic genius. Lucinda, who had been divided between hope and fear as to Roger's possibly marrying,— the fear of a diminished empire having exceeded, on the whole, the hope of company below stairs,—accepted Nora's arrival as a very comfortable compromise. The child was too young to menace her authority, and yet of sufficient importance to warrant a gradual extension of the household economy. Lucinda had a vision of new carpets and curtains, of a regenerated kitchen, of a series of new caps, of her niece coming to sew. Nora was the narrow end of the wedge; it would broaden with her growth. Lucinda therefore was gracious.

For Roger it seemed as if life had begun afresh and the world had put on a new face. High above the level horizon now, clearly defined against the empty sky, rose this small commanding figure, with the added magnitude that objects acquire in this position. She gave him a great deal to think about. The child a man begets and rears weaves its existence insensibly into the tissue of his life so that he becomes trained by fine degrees to the paternal office. But Roger had to skip experience, and spring with a bound into the paternal consciousness. In fact he missed his leap, and never tried again. Time should induct him at leisure into his proper honours, whatever they might be. He felt a strong aversion to claim in the child that prosaic right of property which belongs to the paternal name. He eagerly accepted his novel duties and cares, but he shrank with a tender humility of temper from all precise definition of his rights. He was too young and too sensible of his youth to wish to give this final turn to things. His heart was flattered, rather, by the idea of living at the mercy of change which might always be change for the better. It lay close to his heart, however, to drive away the dusky fears and sordid memories of Nora's anterior life. He strove to conceal the past from her childish sense by a great pictured screen of present joys and comforts. He wished her life to date from the moment he had taken her home. He had taken her for better, for worse; but he longed to quench all baser chances in the daylight of actual security. His philosophy in this as in all things was extremely simple,— to make her happy that she might be good. Meanwhile as he cunningly devised her happiness, his own seemed securely established. He felt twice as much a man as before, and the world seemed as much again a world. All his small stale merits became fragrant with the virtue of unselfish use.

One of his first acts, before he left town, had been to divest Nora of her shabby mourning and dress her afresh in childish colours. He learned from the proprietor's wife at his hotel that this was considered by several ladies interested in Nora's fortunes (especially by her of the subscription) an act of gross impiety; but he held to his purpose, nevertheless. When she was freshly arrayed, he took her to a photographer and made her sit for half a dozen portraits. They were not flattering; they gave her an aged, sombre, lifeless air. He showed them to two old ladies of his acquaintance, whose judgement he valued, without saying whom they represented; the ladies pronounced her a "fright." It was directly after this that Roger hurried her away to the peaceful un-critical country. Her manner here for a long time remained singularly docile and spiritless. She was not exactly sad, but neither was she cheerful. She smiled, as if from the fear to displease by not smiling. She had the air of a child who has been much alone, and who has learned quite to underestimate her natural right to amusement. She seemed at times hopelessly, defiantly torpid. "Heaven help me!" thought Roger, as he surreptitiously watched her; "is she going to be simply stupid?" He perceived at last, however, that her listless quietude covered a great deal of observation, and that growing may be a very soundless process. His ignorance of the past distressed and vexed him, jealous as he was of admitting even to himself that she had ever lived till now. He trod on tiptoe in the region of her early memories, in the dread of reviving some dormant claim, some ugly ghost. Yet he felt that to know so little of her twelve first years was to reckon without an important factor in his problem; as if, in spite of his summons to all the fairies for this second baptism, the godmother-in-chief lurked maliciously apart. Nora seemed by instinct to have perceived the fitness of not speaking of her own affairs, and indeed displayed in the matter a precocious good taste. Among her scanty personal effects the only object referring too vividly to the past had been a small painted photograph of her mother, a languid-looking lady in a low-necked dress, with a good deal of rather crudely rendered prettiness. Nora had apparently a timid reserve of complacency in the fact, which she once imparted to Roger with a kind of desperate abruptness, that her mother had been a public singer; and the heterogeneous nature of her own culture testified to some familiarity with the scenery of Bohemia. The common relations of things seemed quite reversed in her brief experience, and immaturity and precocity shared her young mind in the freest fellowship. She was ignorant of the plainest truths and credulous of the quaintest falsities; unversed in the commonest learning and instructed in the rarest. She barely knew that the earth is round, but she knew that Leonora is the heroine of *Il Trovatore*. She could neither write nor spell, but she could perform the most surprising tricks with cards. She confessed to a passion for strong green tea, and to an interest in the romances of the Sunday newspapers. Evidently she had sprung from a horribly vulgar soil; she was a brand snatched from the burning. She uttered various impolite words with the most guileless accent and glance, and was as yet equally unsuspicious of the grammar and the Catechism. But when once Roger had straightened out her phrase she was careful to preserve its shape; and when he had decimated her vocabulary she made its surviving particles suffice. For the rudiments of theological learning, also, she manifested a due respect. Considering her makeshift education, he wondered she was so much of a lady. His impression of her father was fatal, ineffaceable; the late Mr. Lambert had been a blackguard. Roger had a fancy, however, that this was not all the truth. He was free to assume that the poor fellow's wife had been of a gentle nurture and temper; and he even framed on this theme an ingenious little romance, which gave him a great deal of comfort. Mrs. Lambert had been deceived by the impudent plausibility of her husband, and had come to her senses amid shifting expedients and struggling poverty, during which she had been glad to turn to account the voice which the friends of her happier girlhood had praised. She had died outwearied and broken-hearted, invoking human pity on her child. Roger established in this way a sentimental intimacy with the poor lady's spirit, and exchanged many a greeting over the little girl's head with this vague maternal shape. But he was by no means given up to these thin-spun joys; he gave himself larger satisfactions. He determined to drive in the first nail with his own hands, to lay the smooth foundation-stones of Nora's culture, to teach her to read and write and cipher, to associate himself largely with the growth of her primal sense of things. Behold him thus converted into a gentle pedagogue, prompting her with small caresses and correcting her with smiles. A moted morning sunbeam used to enter his little study, and, resting on Nora's auburn hair, seemed to make of the place a humming school-room. Roger began also to anticipate the future exactions of preceptorship. He plunged into a course of useful reading, and devoured a hundred volumes on education, on hygiene, on morals, on history. He drew up a table of rules and observances for the child's health; he weighed and measured her food, and spent hours with Lucinda, the minister's wife, and the doctor, in the discussion of her regimen and clothing. He bought her a pony, and rode with her over the neighbouring country, roamed with her in the woods and fields, and picked out nice acquaintances for her among the little damsels of the country-side. A doting granddam, in all this matter, could not have shown a finer genius for detail. His zeal indeed left him very little peace, and Lucinda often endeavoured to assuage it by the assurance that he was fretting himself away and wearing himself thin on his happiness. He passed a dozen times a week from the fear of coddling and spoiling the child to the fear of letting her run wild and grow coarse and rustic.

Sometimes he dismissed her tasks for days together, and kept her idling at his side in the winter sunshine; sometimes for a week he kept her within doors, reading to her, preaching to her, showing her prints, and telling her stories. She had an excellent musical ear, and the promise of a charming voice; Roger took counsel in a dozen quarters as to whether he ought to make her use her voice or spare it. Once he took her up to town to a *matinée* at one of the theatres, and was in anguish for a week afterwards, lest he had quickened some inherited tendency to dissipation. He used to lie awake at night, trying hard to fix in his mind the happy medium between coldness and weak fondness. With a heart full of tenderness, he used to measure out his caresses. He was in doubt for a long time as to what he should make her call him. At the outset he decided instinctively against "papa." It was a question between "Mr. Lawrence" and his baptismal name. He weighed the proprieties for a week, and then he determined the child should choose for herself. She had as yet avoided addressing him by name; at last he asked what name she preferred. She stared rather blankly at the time, but a few days afterwards he heard her shouting "Roger!" from the garden under his window. She had ventured upon a small shallow pond enclosed by his land, and now coated with thin ice. The ice had cracked with a great report under her tread, and was swaying gently beneath her weight, at some yards from the edge. In her alarm her heart had chosen, and her heart's election was never subsequently gainsaid. Circumstances seemed to affect her slowly; for a long time she showed few symptoms of change. Roger in his slippers, by the fireside, in the winter evenings, used to gaze at her with an anxious soul, and wonder whether it was not only a stupid child that could sit for an hour by the chimney-corner, stroking the cat's back in absolute silence, asking neither questions nor favours. Then, meeting her intelligent eyes, he would fancy that she was wiser than he knew; that she was mocking him or judging him, and counterplotting his pious labours with elfish subtlety. Arrange it as he might, he could not call her pretty. Plain women are apt to be clever; might she not (horror of horrors!) turn out too clever? In the evening, after she had attended Nora to bed, Lucinda would come into the little library, and she and Roger would solemnly put their heads together. In matters in which he deemed her sex gave her an advantage of judgement, he used freely to ask her opinion. She made a great parade of motherly science, rigid spinster as she was, and hinted by many a nod and wink at the mystic depths of her sagacity. As to the child's being thankless or heartless, she quite reassured him. Didn't she cry herself to sleep, under her breath, on her little pillow? Didn't she mention him every night in her prayers,—him, and him alone? However much her family may have left to be desired as a "family,"—and of its shortcomings in this respect Lucinda had an altogether awful sense,—Nora was clearly a lady in her own right. As for her plain face, they could wait awhile for a change. Plainness in a child was almost always prettiness in a woman; and at all events, if she was not to be pretty, she need never be proud.

Roger had no wish to remind his young companion of what she owed him; for it was the very keystone of his plan that their relation should ripen into a perfect matter of course; but he watched patiently, as a wandering botanist for the first woodland violets for the year, for the shy field-flower of spontaneous affection. He aimed at nothing more or less than to inspire the child with a passion. Until he had detected in her glance and tone the note of passionate tenderness his experiment must have failed. It would have succeeded on the day when she should break out into cries and tears and tell him with a clinging embrace that she loved him. So he argued with himself; but, in fact, he expected perhaps more than belongs to the lame logic of this life. As a child, she would be too irreflective to play so pretty a part; as a young girl, too self-conscious. I undertake, however, to tell no secrets. Roger, being by nature undemonstrative, continued to possess his soul in patience. Nora, meanwhile, seemingly showed as little of distrust as of positive tenderness. She grew and grew in ungrudged serenity. It was in person, first, that she began gently, or rather ungently, to expand; acquiring a well-nurtured sturdiness of contour, but passing quite into the shambling and sheepish stage of girlhood. Lucinda cast about her in vain for possibilities of future beauty, and took refuge in vigorous attention to the young girl's bountiful auburn hair, which she combed and braided with a kind of fierce assiduity. The winter had passed away, the spring was well advanced. Roger, looking at the object of his adoption, felt a certain sinking of the heart as he thought of his cousin Hubert's visit. As matters stood, Nora bore rather livelier testimony to his charity than to his taste.

He had debated some time as to whether he should write to Hubert and as to how he should write. Hubert Lawrence was some four years his junior; but Roger had always allowed him a large precedence in the things of the mind. Hubert had just commenced parson; it seemed now that grace would surely lend a generous hand to nature and complete the circle of his accomplishments. He was extremely good-looking and clever with just such a cleverness as seemed but an added personal charm. He and Roger had been much together in early life and had formed an intimacy strangely compounded of harmony and discord. Utterly unlike in temper and tone, they neither thought nor felt nor acted together on any single point. Roger was constantly differing, mutely and profoundly, and Hubert frankly and sarcastically; but each, nevertheless, seemed to find in the other an irritating counterpart and complement. They had between them a kind of boyish levity which kept them from lingering long on delicate ground; but they felt at times that they belonged, by temperament, to irreconcilable camps, and that the more each of them came to lead his own life, the more their lives would diverge. Roger was of a loving turn of mind, and it cost him many a sigh that a certain glassy hardness of soul on his cousin's part was for ever blunting the edge of his affection. He nevertheless had a deep regard for Hubert; he admired his talents, he enjoyed his society, he wrapped him about with his good-will. He had told him more than once that he cared for him more than Hubert would ever believe, could in the nature of things believe. He was willing to take his cousin seriously, even when he knew his cousin was not taking him so. Hubert, who reserved his faith for heavenly mysteries, had small credence for earthly ones, and he would have affirmed that to his perception they loved each other with a precisely equal ardour, beyond everything in life, to wit, but themselves. Roger had in his mind a kind of metaphysical "idea" of a possible Hubert, which the actual Hubert took a wanton satisfaction in turning upside down. Roger had drawn in his fancy a pure and ample outline, into which the young ecclesiastic projected a perversely ill-fitting shadow. Roger took his cousin more seriously than the young man took himself. In fact, Hubert had apparently come into the world to play. He played at life, altogether; he played at learning, he played at theology, he played at friendship; and it was to be conjectured that, on particular holidays, he would play pretty hard at love. Hubert, for some time, had been settled in New York, and of late they had exchanged but few letters. Something had been said about Hubert's coming to spend a part of his summer vacation with his cousin; now that the latter was at the head of a household and a family, Roger reminded him of their understanding. He had finally told him his little romance, with a fine bravado of indifference to his verdict; but he was, in secret, extremely anxious to obtain Hubert's judgement of the heroine. Hubert replied that he was altogether prepared for the news, and that it must be a very pretty sight to see him at dinner pinning her bib, or to hear him sermonising her over a torn frock.

"But, pray, what relation is the young lady to me?" he added. "How far does the adoption go, and where does it stop? Your own proper daughter would be my cousin; but you can't adopt for other people. I shall wait till I see her; then if she is pleasing, I shall admit her into cousinship."

He came down for a fortnight, in July, and was soon introduced to Nora. She came sidling shyly into the room, with a rent in her short-waisted frock, and the *Child's Own Book* in her hand, with her finger in the history of *The Discreet Princess*. Hubert kissed her gallantly, and declared that he was happy to make her acquaintance. She retreated to a station beside Roger's knee, and stood staring at the young man. "*Elle a les pieds énormes,*" said Hubert.

Roger was annoyed, partly with himself, for he made her wear big shoes. "What do you think of him?" he asked, stroking the child's hair, and hoping, half maliciously, that, with the frank perspicacity of childhood, she would make some inspired "hit" about the young man. But to appreciate Hubert's failings, one must have had vital experience of them. At this time, twenty-five years of age, he was a singularly handsome youth. Although of about the same height as his cousin, the pliant slimness of his figure made him look taller. He had a cool blue eye and clustering yellow locks. His features were cut with admirable purity; his teeth were white, his smile superb. "I think," said Nora, "that he looks like the *Prince Avenant.*"

Before Hubert went away, Roger asked him for a deliberate opinion of the child. Was she ugly or pretty? was she interesting? He found it hard, however, to induce him to consider her seriously. Hubert's observation was exercised rather less in the interest of general truth than of particular profit; and of what profit to Hubert was Nora's shambling childhood? "I can't think of her as a girl," he said; "she seems to me a boy. She climbs trees, she scales fences, she keeps rabbits, she straddles upon your old mare. I found her this morning wading in the pond. She is growing up a hoyden; you ought to give her more civilising influences than she enjoys hereabouts; you ought to engage a governess, or send her to school. It is well enough now; but, my poor fellow, what will you do when she is twenty?"

You may imagine, from Hubert's sketch, that Nora's was a happy life. She had few companions, but during the long summer days, in woods and fields and orchards, Roger initiated her into all those rural mysteries which are so dear to childhood and so fondly remembered in later years. She grew more hardy and lively, more inquisitive, more active. She tasted deeply of the joy of tattered dresses and sun-burnt cheeks and arms, and long nights at the end of tired days. But Roger, pondering his cousin's words began to believe that to keep her longer at home would be to fail of justice to the *ewig Weibliche*. The current of her growth would soon begin to flow deeper than the plummet of a man's wit. He determined, therefore to send her to school, and he began with this view to investigate the merits of various seminaries. At last, after a vast amount of meditation and an extensive correspondence with the school-keeping class, he selected one which appeared rich in fair promises. Nora, who had never known an hour's schooling, entered joyously upon her new career; but she gave her friend that sweet and long-deferred emotion of which I have spoken, when, on parting with him, she hung upon his neck with a sort of convulsive fondness. He took her head in his two hands and looked at her; her eyes were streaming with tears. During the month which followed he received from her a dozen letters, sadly misspelled, but divinely lachrymose.

It is needless to relate in detail this phase of Nora's history, which lasted two years. Roger found that he missed her sadly; his occupation was gone. Still, her very absence occupied him. He wrote her long letters of advice, told her everything that happened to him, and sent her books and useful garments, biscuits and oranges. At the end of a year he began to long terribly to take her back again; but as his judgement forbade this measure, he determined to beguile the following year by travel. Before starting, he went to the little country town which was the seat of her academy, to bid Nora farewell. He had not seen her since she left him, as he had chosen— quite heroically, poor fellow—to have her spend her vacation with a schoolmate, the bosom friend of this especial period. He found her surprisingly altered. She looked three years older; she was growing by the hour. Prettiness and symmetry had not yet been vouchsafed to her; but Roger found in her young imperfection a sweet assurance that her account with nature was not yet closed.

She had, moreover, an elusive grace. She had reached that charming girlish moment when the crudity of childhood begins to be faintly tempered by the sense of sex. She was coming fast, too, into her woman's heritage of garrulity. She entertained him for a whole morning; she took him into her confidence; she rattled and prattled unceasingly upon all the swarming little school interests, —her likes and aversions, her hopes and fears, her friends and teachers, her studies and story-books. Roger sat grinning in high enchantment; she seemed to him the very genius of girlhood. For the very first time, he became conscious of her character; there was an immense deal of her; she overflowed. When they parted, he gave his hopes to her keeping in a long, long kiss. She kissed him too, but this time with smiles, not with tears. She neither suspected nor could she have understood the thought which, during this interview, had blossomed in her friend's mind. On leaving her, he took a long walk in the country over unknown roads. That evening he consigned his thought to a short letter, addressed to Mrs. Keith. This was the present title of the lady who had once been Miss Morton. She had married and gone abroad, where, in Rome, she had done as the Americans do, and entered the Roman Church. His letter ran as follows:—

My dear Mrs. Keith—I promised you once to be very unhappy, but I doubt whether you believed me; you did not look as if you believed me. I am sure, at all events, you hoped otherwise. I am told you have become a Roman Catholic. Perhaps you have been praying for me at St. Peter's. This is the easiest way to account for my conversion to a worthier state of mind. You know that, two years ago, I adopted a homeless little girl. One of these days she will be a lovely woman. I mean to do what I can to make her one. Perhaps, six years hence, she will be grateful enough not to refuse me as you did. Pray for me more than ever. I have begun at the beginning; it will be my own fault if I have not a perfect wife.

III

ROGER's journey was long and various. He went to the West Indies and to South America, whence, taking a ship at one of the eastern ports, he sailed round the Horn and paid a visit to Mexico. He journeyed thence to California, and returned home across the Isthmus, stopping awhile on his upward course at various Southern cities. It was in some degree a sentimental journey. Roger was a practical man; as he went he gathered facts and noted manners and customs; but the muse of observation for him was the little girl at home, the ripening companion of his own ripe years. It was for her sake that he collected impressions and laid up treasure. He had determined that she should be a lovely woman and a perfect wife; but to be worthy of such a woman as his fancy foreshadowed, he himself had much to learn. To be a good husband, one must first be a wise man; to educate her, he should first educate himself. He would make it possible that daily contact with him should be a liberal education, and that his simple society should be a benefit. For this purpose he should be a fountain of knowledge, a compendium of experience. He travelled in a spirit of solemn attention, like some grim devotee of a former age making a pilgrimage for the welfare of one he loved. He kept with great labour a copious diary, which he meant to read aloud on the winter nights of coming years. His diary was directly addressed to Nora, she being implied throughout as reader or auditor. He thought at moments of his vow to Isabel Morton, and asked himself what had become of the passion of that hour. It had betaken itself to the common limbo of our dead passions. He rejoiced to know that she was well and happy; he meant to write to her again on his return and tell her that he himself was as happy as she could wish to see him. He mused ever and anon on the nature of his affection for Nora, and wondered what earthly name he could call it by. Assuredly he was not in love with her: you could not fall in love with a child. But if he had not a lover's love, he had at least a lover's jealousy; it would have made him miserable to believe his scheme might miscarry. It would fail, he fondly assured himself, by no fault of hers. He was sure of her future; in that last interview at school he had guessed the answer to the riddle of her formless girlhood. If he could only be as sure of his own constancy as of hers! On this point poor Roger might fairly have let his conscience rest; but to test his resolution, he deliberately courted temptation, and on a dozen occasions allowed present loveliness to measure itself with absent promise. At the risk of a large expenditure of blushes, he bravely incurred the blandishments of various charming persons of the South. They failed signally, in every case but one, to quicken his pulses. He studied these gracious persons, he noted their gifts and graces, so that he might know the range of the feminine charm. Of the utmost that women can be and do he wished to have personal experience. But with the sole exception I have mentioned, not a syren of them all but shone with a radiance less magical than that dim but rounded shape which glimmered for ever in the dark future, like the luminous complement of the early moon. It was at Lima that his poor little potential Nora suffered temporary eclipse. He made here the acquaintance of a young Spanish lady whose plump and full-blown innocence seemed to him divinely amiable. If ignorance is grace, what a lamentable folly to be wise! He had crossed from Havana to Rio on the same vessel with her brother, a friendly young fellow, who had made him promise to come and stay with him on his arrival at Lima. Roger, in execution of this promise, passed three weeks under his roof, in the society of the lovely Teresita. She caused him to reflect, with a good deal of zeal. She moved him the more because, being wholly without coquetry, she made no attempt whatever to interest him. Her charm was the charm of absolute naïveté, and a certain tame unseasoned sweetness,—the sweetness of an angel who is without mundane reminiscences; to say nothing of a pair of liquid hazel eyes and a coil of crinkled blue-black hair. She could barely write her name, and from the summer twilight of her mind, which seemed to ring with amorous bird-notes, she flung a disparaging shadow upon Nora's prospective condition. Roger thought of Nora, by contrast, as a kind of superior doll, a thing wound up with a key, whose virtues would make a *tic-tic* if one listened. Why travel so far about for a wife, when here was one ready made to his heart, as illiterate as an angel, and as faithful as the little page of a medieval ballad,—and with those two perpetual love-lights beneath her silly little forehead?

Day by day, near the pretty Peruvian, Roger grew better pleased with the present. It was so happy, so idle, so secure! He protested against the future. He grew impatient of the stiff little figure which he had posted in the distance, to stare at him with those monstrous pale eyes; they seemed to grow and grow as he thought of them. In other words, he was in love with Teresa. She, on her side, was delighted to be loved. She caressed him with her fond dark looks and smiled perpetual assent. Late one afternoon they ascended together to a terrace on the top of the house. They sun had just disappeared; the southern landscape was drinking in the cool of night. They stood awhile in silence; at last Roger felt that he must speak of his love. He walked away to the farther end of the terrace, casting about in his mind for the fitting words. They were hard to find. His companion spoke a little English, and he a little Spanish; but there came upon him a sudden perplexing sense of the infantine rarity of her wits. He had never done her the honour to pay her a compliment, he had never really talked with her. It was not for him to talk, but for her to perceive! She turned about, leaning back against the parapet of the terrace, looking at him and smiling. She was always smiling. She had on an old faded pink morning dress, very much open at the throat, and a ribbon round her neck to which was suspended a little cross of turquoise. One of the braids of her hair had fallen down, and she had drawn it forward, and was plaiting the end with her plump white fingers. Her nails were not fastidiously clean. He went towards her. When he next became perfectly conscious of their relative positions, he knew that he had tenderly kissed her, more than once, and that she had more than suffered him. He stood holding both her hands; he was blushing; her own complexion was undisturbed, her smile barely deepened; another of her braids had come down. He was filled with a sense of pleasure in her sweetness, tempered by a vague feeling of pain in his all-too-easy conquest. There was nothing of poor Teresita but that you could kiss her! It came upon him with a sort of horror that he had never yet distinctly told her that he loved her. "Teresa," he said, almost angrily, "I love you. Do you understand?" For all answer she raised his two hands successively to her lips. Soon after this she went off with her mother to church.

The next morning, one of his friend's clerks brought him a package of letters from his banker. One of them was a note from Nora. It ran as follows:—

DEAR ROGER—I want so much to tell you that I have just got the prize for the piano. I hope you will not think it very silly to write so far only to tell you this. But I am so proud I want you to know it. Of the three girls who tried for it, two were seventeen. The prize is a beautiful picture called "Mozart à Vienne"; probably you have seen it. Miss Murray says I may hang it up in my bedroom. Now I have got to go and practise, for Miss Murray says I must practise more than ever. My dear Roger, I do hope you are enjoying your travels. I have learned a great deal of geography, following you on the map. Don't ever forget your loving

NORA.

After reading this letter, Roger told his host that he

should have to leave him. The young Peruvian de-murred, objected, and begged for a reason.

"Well," said Roger, "I find I am in love with your sister." The words sounded on his ear as if some one else had spoken them. Teresita's light was quenched, and she had no more fascination than a smouldering lamp, smelling of oil.

"Why, my dear fellow," said his friend, "that seems to me a reason for staying. I shall be most happy to have you for a brother-in-law."

"It's impossible! I am engaged to a young lady in my own country."

"You are in love here, you are engaged there, and you go where you are engaged! You Englishmen are strange fellows!"

"Tell Teresa that I adore her, but that I am pledged at home. I would rather not see her."

And so Roger departed from Lima, without further communion with Teresita. On his return home he received a letter from her brother, telling him of her engagement to a young merchant of Valparaiso,—an excellent match. The young lady sent him her salutations. Roger, answering his friend's letter, begged that the Doña Teresa would accept, as a wedding present, of the accompanying trinket,—a little brooch in turquoise. It would look very well with pink!

Roger reached home in the autumn, but left Nora at school till the beginning of the Christmas holidays. He occupied the interval in refurnishing his house, and clearing the stage for the last act of the young girl's childhood. He had always possessed a modest taste for upholstery; he now began to apply it under the guidance of a delicate idea. His idea led him to prefer, in all things, the fresh and graceful to the grave and formal, and to wage war throughout his old dwelling on the lurking mustiness of the past. He had a lively regard for elegance, balanced by a horror of wanton luxury. He fancied that a woman is the better for being well dressed and well domiciled, and that vanity, too stingily treated, is sure to avenge itself. So he took vanity into account. Nothing annoyed him more, however, than the fear of seeing Nora a precocious fine lady; so that while he aimed at all possible purity of effect, he stayed his hand here and there before certain admonitory relics of ancestral ugliness and virtue, embodied for the most part in haircloth and cotton damask. Chintz and muslin, flowers and photographs and books, gave their clear light tone to the house. Nothing could be more tenderly propitious and virginal, or better chosen both to chasten the young girl's aspirations and to remind her of her protector's tenderness.

Since his return he had designedly refused himself a glimpse of her. He wished to give her a single undivided welcome to his home and his heart. Shortly before Christmas, as he had even yet not set his house in order, Lucinda Brown was sent to fetch her from school. If Roger had expected that Nora would return with any striking accession of beauty, he would have had to say "Amen" with an effort. She had pretty well ceased to be a child; she was still his grave, imperfect Nora. She had gained her full height,—a great height, which her young strong slimness rendered the more striking. Her slender throat supported a head of massive mould, bound about with dense auburn braids. Beneath a somewhat serious brow her large, fair eyes retained their collected light, as if uncertain where to fling it. Now and then the lids parted widely and showered down these gathered shafts; and if at these times a certain rare smile divided, in harmony, her childish lips, Nora was for the moment a passable beauty. But for the most part, the best charm of her face was in a modest refinement of line, which rather evaded notice than courted it. The first impression she was likely to produce was of a kind of awkward slender majesty. Roger pronounced her "stately," and for a fortnight thought her too imposing by half; but as the days went on, and the pliable innocence of early maidenhood gave a soul to this formidable grace, he began to feel that in essentials she was still the little daughter of his charity. He even began to observe in her an added consciousness of this lowly position; as if with the growth of her mind she had come to reflect upon it, and deem it less and less a matter of course. He meditated much as to whether he should frankly talk it over with her and allow her to feel that, for him as well, their relation could never become commonplace. This would be in a measure untender, but would it not be prudent? Ought he not, in the interest of his final purpose, to infuse into her soul in her sensitive youth an impression of all that she owed him, so that when his time had come, if her imagination should lead her a-wandering, gratitude would stay her steps? A dozen times over he was on the verge of making his point, of saying, "Nora, Nora, these are not vulgar alms; I expect a return. One of these days you must pay your debt. Guess my riddle! I love you less than you think—and more! A word to the wise." But he was silenced by a saving sense of the brutality of such a course and by a suspicion that, after all, it was not needful. A passion of gratitude was silently gathering in the young girl's heart: that heart could be trusted to keep its engagements. A deep conciliatory purpose seemed now to pervade her life, of infinite delight to Roger as little by little it stole upon his mind like the fragrance of a deepening spring. He had his idea; he suspected that she had hers. They were but opposite faces of the same deep need. Her musing silence, her deliberate smiles, the childish keenness of her questionings, the delicacy of her little nameless services and caresses, were all a kind of united acknowledgment and promise.

On Christmas eve they sat together alone by a blazing log-fire in Roger's little library. He had been reading aloud a chapter of his diary, to which Nora sat listening in dutiful demureness, though her thoughts evidently were nearer home than Cuba and Peru. There is no denying it was dull; he could gossip to better purpose. He felt its dullness himself and closing it finally with good-humoured petulance, declared it was fit only to throw into the fire. Upon which Nora looked up, protesting. "You must do no such thing," she said. "You must keep your journals carefully, and one of these days I shall have them bound in morocco and gilt, and ranged in a row in my own book-case."

"That is but a polite way of burning them up," said Roger. "They will be as little read as if they were in the fire. I don't know how it is. They seemed to be very amusing when I wrote them; they are as stale as an old newspaper now. I can't write: that's the amount of it. I am a very stupid fellow, Nora; you might as well know it first as last."

Nora's school had been of the punctilious Episcopal order, and she had learned there the pretty custom of decorating the house at Christmas-tide with garlands and crowns of evergreen and holly. She had spent the day in decking out the chimney-piece, and now, seated on a stool under the mantel-shelf, she twisted the last little wreath which was to complete her design. A great still snow-storm was falling without, and seemed to be blocking them in from the world. She bit off the thread with which she had been binding her twigs, held out her garland to admire its effect, and then, "I don't believe you are stupid, Roger," she said; "and if I did, I should not much care."

"Is that philosophy or indifference?" said the young man.

"I don't know that it's either; it's because I know you are so good."

"That is what they say about all stupid people."

Nora added another twig to her wreath and bound it up. "I am sure," she said at last, "that when people are as good as you are, they cannot be stupid. I should like some one to tell me you are stupid. I know, Roger; *I* know!"

The young man began to feel a little uneasy; it was no part of his plan that her good-will should spend itself too soon. "Dear me, Nora, if you think so well of me, I shall find it hard to live up to your expectations. I am afraid I shall disappoint you. I have a little gimcrack to put in your stocking to-night; but I'm rather ashamed of it now."

"A gimcrack more or less is of small account. I have had my stocking hanging up these three years, and everything I possess is a present from you."

Roger frowned; the conversation had taken just such a turn as he had often longed to provoke, but now it was disagreeable to him. "O come," he said; "I have done simply my duty to my little girl."

"But Roger," said Nora, staring with expanded eyes, "I am not your little girl."

His frown darkened; his heart began to beat. "Don't talk nonsense!" he said.

"But, Roger, it is true. I am no one's little girl. Do you think I have no memory? Where is my father? Where is my mother?"

"Listen to me," said Roger sternly. "You must not talk of such things."

"You must not forbid me, Roger. I can't think of them without thinking of you. This is Christmas eve! Miss Murray told us that we must never let it pass without thinking of all that it means. But without Miss Murray, I have been thinking all day of things which are hard to name,—of death and life, of my parents and you, of my incredible happiness. I feel to-night like a princess in a fairy-tale. I am a poor creature, without a friend, without a penny or a home; and yet, here I sit by a blazing fire, with money, with food, with clothes, with love. The snow outside is burying the stone walls, and yet here I can sit and simply say, 'How pretty!' Suppose I were in it, wandering and begging,—I might have been! Should I think it pretty then? Roger, Roger, I am no one's child!" The tremor in her voice deepened, and she broke into a sudden passion of tears. Roger took her in his arms and tried to soothe away her sobs. But she disengaged herself and went on with an almost fierce exaltation: "No, no, I won't be comforted! I have had comfort enough; I hate it. I want for an hour to be myself and feel how little that is, to be my miserable father's daughter, to fancy I hear my mother's voice. I have never spoken of them before; you must let me to-night. You must tell me about my father; you know something. I don't. You never refused me anything, Roger; don't refuse me this. He was not good, like you; but now he can do no harm. You have never mentioned his name to me, but happy as we are here together, we ought not,—we ought not, to despise him!"

Roger yielded to the vehemence of this flood of emotion. He stood watching her with two helpless tears in his own eyes, and then he drew her gently towards him and kissed her on the forehead. She took up her work again, and he told her, with every minutest detail he could recall, the story of his sole brief interview with Mr. Lambert. Gradually he lost the sense of effort and reluctance, and talked freely, abundantly, almost with pleasure.

Nora listened very solemnly,—with an amount of self-control which denoted the habit of constant retrospect. She asked a hundred questions as to Roger's impression of her father's appearance. Was he not wonderfully handsome? Then taking up the tale herself, she poured out a torrent of feverish reminiscence. She disinterred her early memories with a kind of rapture of relief. Her evident joy in this frolic of confidence gave Roger a pitying sense of what her long silence must have cost her. But evidently she bore him no grudge, and his present tolerance of her rambling gossip seemed to her but another proof of his charity. She rose at last, and stood before the fire, into which she had thrown the refuse of her greenery, watching it blaze up and turn to ashes. "So much for the past!" she said at last. "The rest is the future. The girls at school used to be always talking about what they meant to do in coming years, what they hoped, what they wished; wondering, choosing, imagining. You don't know how girls talk, Roger: you would be surprised! I never used to say much: my future is fixed. I have nothing to choose, nothing to hope, nothing to fear. I am to make you happy. That's simple enough. You have undertaken to bring me up, Roger; you must do your best, because now I am here, it's for long, and you would rather have a wise girl than a silly one." And she smiled with a kind of tentative daughterliness through the traces of her recent grief. She put her two hands on his shoulders and eyed him with conscious gravity. "You shall never repent. I shall learn everything. I shall be everything! Oh! I wish I were pretty." And she tossed back her head, in impatience of her fatal plainness, with an air which forced Roger to assure her that she would do very well as she was. "If you are satisfied," she said, "I am!" For a moment Roger felt as if she were twenty years old.

This serious Christmas eve left its traces upon many ensuing weeks. Nora's education was resumed with a certain added solemnity. Roger was no longer obliged to condescend to the level of her intelligence, and he found reason to thank his stars that he had improved his own mind. He found use for all the knowledge he possessed. The day of childish "lessons" was over, and Nora sought instruction in the perusal of various classical authors, in her own and other tongues, in concert with her friend. They read aloud to each other alternately, discussed their acquisitions, and digested them with perhaps equal rapidity. Roger, in former years, had had but a small literary appetite; he liked a few books and knew them well, but he felt as if to settle down to an unread author were very like starting on a journey,— a case for farewells, packing trunks, and buying tickets. His curiosity, now, however, imbued and quickened with a motive, led him through a hundred untrodden paths. He found it hard sometimes to keep pace with Nora's pattering step; through the flowery lanes of poetry, in especial, she would gallop without drawing breath. Was she quicker-witted than her friend, or only more superficial? Something of one, doubtless, and something of the other. Roger was for ever suspecting her of a deeper penetration than his own, and hanging his head with an odd mixture of pride and humility. Her quick perception, at times, made him feel irretrievably dull and antiquated. His ears would tingle, his cheeks would burn, his old hope would fade into a shadow. "It's worse than useless," he would declare. "How can I ever have for her that charm of infallibility, that romance of omniscience, that a woman demands of her lover? She has seen me scratching my head, she has seen me counting on my fingers! Before she is seventeen she will be mortally tired of me, and by the time she is twenty I shall be fatally familiar and incurably stale. It's very well for her to talk about life-long devotion and eternal gratitude. She doesn't know the meaning of words. She must grow and outgrow, that is her first necessity. She must come to woman's estate and pay the inevitable tribute. I can open the door and let in the lover. If she loves me now I shall have had my turn. I can't hope to be the object of two passions. I must thank the Lord for small favours!" Then as he seemed to taste, in advance, the bitterness of disappointment, casting about him angrily for some means of appeal: "I ought to go away and stay away for years and never write at all, instead of compounding ponderous diaries to make even my absence detestable. I ought to convert myself into a beneficent shadow, a vague tutelary name. Then I ought to come back in glory, fragrant with exotic perfumes and shod with shoes of mystery! Otherwise, I ought to clip the wings of her fancy and put her on half-rations. I ought to snub her and scold her and bully her and tell her she's deplorably plain,—treat her as Rochester treats Jane Eyre. If I were only a good old Catholic, that I might shut her up in a convent and keep her childish and stupid and contented!" Roger felt that he was too doggedly conscientious; but abuse his conscience as he would, he could not make it yield an inch; so that in the constant strife between his egotistical purpose and his generous temper, the latter kept gaining ground, and Nora innocently enjoyed the spoils of victory. It was his very generosity that detained him on the spot, by her side, watching her, working for her, performing a hundred offices which other hands would have but scanted. Roger watched intently for the signs of that inevitable hour when a young girl begins to loosen her fingers in the grasp of a guiding hand and wander softly in pursuit of the sinuous silver thread which deflects, through meadows of perennial green, from the dull grey stream of the common lot. She had relapsed in the course of time into the careless gaiety and the light, immediate joys of girlhood. If she cherished a pious purpose in her heart, she made no indecent parade of it. But her very placidity and patience somehow afflicted her friend. She was too monotonously sweet, too easily obedient. If once in a while she would only flash out into petulance or rebellion! She kept her temper so carefully: what in the world was she keeping it for? If she would only bless him for once with an angry look and tell him that he bored her!

During the second year after her return from school Roger began to imagine that she avoided his society and resented his attentions. She was fond of lonely walks, readings, reveries. She was fond of novels, and she read a great many. For works of fiction in general Roger had no great relish, though he confessed to three or four old-fashioned favourites. These were not always Nora's. One evening in the early spring she sat down to a twentieth perusal of the classic tale of *The Heir of Redclyffe*. Roger, as usual, asked her to read aloud. She began, and proceeded through a dozen pages. Looking up, at this point, she beheld Roger asleep. She smiled softly, and privately resumed her reading. At the end of an hour, Roger, having finished his nap, rather startled her by his excessive annoyance at his lapse of consciousness. He wondered whether he had snored, but the absurd fellow was ashamed to ask her. Recovering himself finally, "The fact is, Nora," he said, "all novels seem to me stupid. They are nothing to what *I* can fancy! I have in my heart a prettier romance than any of them."

"A romance?" said Nora simply. "Pray let me hear it. You are quite as good a hero as this stick of a Philip. Begin!"

He stood before the fire, looking at her with almost funereal gravity. "My dénouement is not yet written," he said. "Wait till the story is finished; then you shall hear the whole."

As at this time Nora put on long dresses and began to arrange her hair as a young lady, it occurred to Roger that he might make some change in his own appearance and reinforce his waning attractions. He was now thirty-three; he fancied he was growing stout. Bald, corpulent, middle-aged,—at this rate he should soon be shelved! He was seized with a mad desire to win back the lost graces of youth. He had a dozen interviews with his tailor, the result of which was that for a fortnight he appeared daily in a new garment. Suddenly, amid this restless longing to revise and embellish himself, he determined to suppress his whiskers. This would take off five years. He appeared, therefore, one morning, in the severe simplicity of a moustache. Nora started, and greeted him with a little cry of horror. "Don't you like it?" he asked.

She hung her head on one side and the other "Well, no, —to be frank."

"O, of course to be frank! It will only take five years to grow them again. What is the trouble?"

She gave a critical frown. "It makes you look too,— too fat; too much like Mr. Vose." It is sufficient to explain that Mr. Vose was the butcher, who called every day in his cart, and who recently—Roger with horror only now remembered it—had sacrificed his whiskers to a mysterious ideal.

"I am sorry!" said Roger. "It was for you I did it!"

"For me!" And Nora burst into a violent laugh.

"Why, my dear Nora," cried the young man with a certain angry vehemence, "don't I do everything in life for you?"

She became grave again. Then, after much meditation, "Excuse my unfeeling levity," she said. "You might cut off your nose, Roger, and I should like your face as well." But this was but half comfort. "Too fat!" Her subtler sense had spoken, and Roger never encountered Mr. Vose for three months after this without wishing to attack him with one of his own cleavers.

He made now an heroic attempt to scale the frowning

battlements of the future. He pretended to be making arrangements for a tour in Europe, and for having his house completely remodelled in his absence; noting the while attentively the effect upon Nora of his cunning machinations. But she gave no sign of suspicion that his future, to the uttermost day, could be anything but her future too. One evening, nevertheless, an incident occurred which fatally confounded his calculations,—an evening of perfect mid-spring, full of warm, vague odours, of growing daylight, of the sense of bursting sap and fresh-turned earth. Roger sat on the piazza, looking out on these things with an opera-glass. Nora, who had been strolling in the garden, returned to the house and sat down on the steps of the portico. "Roger," she said, after a pause, "has it never struck you as very strange that we should be living together in this way?"

Roger's heart rose to this throat. But he was loath to concede anything, lest he should concede too much. "It is not especially strange," he said.

"Surely it *is* strange," she answered. "What are you? Neither my brother, nor my father, nor my uncle, nor my cousin,—nor even, by law, my guardian."

"By law! My dear child, what do you know about law?"

"I know that if I should run away and leave you now, you could not force me to return."

"That's fine talk! Who told you that?"

"No one; I thought of it myself. As I grow older, I ought to think of such things."

"Upon my word! Of running away and leaving me?"

"That is but one side of the question. The other is that you can turn me out of your house this moment, and no one can force you to take me back. I ought to remember such things."

"Pray what good will it do you to remember them?"

Nora hesitated a moment. "There is always some good in not losing sight of the truth."

"The truth! You are very young to begin to talk about the truth."

"Not too young. I am old for my age. I ought to be!" These last words were uttered with a little sigh which roused Roger to action.

"Since we are talking about the truth," he said. "I wonder whether you know a tithe of it."

For an instant she was silent; then, rising slowly to her feet, "What do you mean?" she asked. "Is there any secret in all that you have done for me?" Suddenly she clasped her hands, and eagerly, with a smile, went on: "You said the other day you had a romance. Is it a real romance, Roger? Are you, after all, related to me,—my cousin, my brother?"

He let her stand before him, perplexed and expectant. "It is more of a romance than that."

She slid upon her knees at his feet. "Dear Roger, do tell me," she said.

He began to stroke her hair. "You think so much," he answered; "do you never think about the future, the real future; ten years hence?"

"A great deal."

"What do you think?"

She blushed a little, and then he felt that she was drawing confidence from his face. "Promise not to laugh!" she said, half laughing herself. He nodded. "I think about my husband!" she proclaimed. And then, as if she had, after all, been very absurd, and to forestall his laughter, "And about your wife!" she quickly added. "I want dreadfully to see her. Why don't you marry?"

He continued to stroke her hair in silence. At last he said sententiously, "I hope to marry one of these days."

"I wish you would do it now," Nora went on. "If only she would be nice! We should be sisters, and I should take care of the children."

"You are too young to understand what you say, or what I mean. Little girls should not talk about marriage. It can mean nothing to you until you come yourself to marry,—as you will, of course. You will have to decide and choose."

"I suppose I shall. I shall refuse him."

"What do you mean?"

But, without answering his question, "Were you ever in love, Roger?" she suddenly asked. "Is that your romance?"

"Almost."

"Then it is not about me, after all?"

"It is about you, Nora; but, after all, it is not a romance. It is solid, it is real, it is truth itself; as true as your silly novels are false. Nora, I care for no one, I shall never care for any one, but you!"

He spoke in tones so deep and solemn that she was

impressed. "Do you mean, Roger, that you care so much for me that you will never marry?"

He rose quickly in his chair, pressing his hand over his brow. "Ah, Nora," he cried, "you are very painful!"

If she had annoyed him she was very contrite. She took his two hands in her own. "Roger," she whispered gravely, "if you don't wish it, I promise never, never, never to marry, but to be yours alone,—yours alone!"

IV

THE summer passed away; Nora was turned sixteen. Deeming it time she should begin to see something of the world, Roger spent the autumn in travelling. Of his tour in Europe he had ceased to talk; it was indefinitely deferred. It matters little where they went; Nora greatly enjoyed the excursion, and found all spots alike delightful. To Roger himself it gave a great deal of comfort. Whether or no his companion was pretty, people certainly looked at her. He overheard them a dozen times call her "striking." *Striking!* The word seemed to him rich in meaning; if he had seen her for the first time taking the breeze on the deck of a river steamer, he certainly should have been struck. On his return home he found among his letters the following missive:—

MY DEAR SIR—I have learned, after various fruitless researches, that you have adopted my cousin. Miss Lambert, at the time she left St. Louis, was too young to know much about her family, or even to care much; and you, I suppose, have not investigated the subject. You, however, better than any one, can understand my desire to make her acquaintance. I hope you will not deny me the privilege. I am the second son of a half-sister of her mother, between whom and my own mother there was always the greatest affection. It was not until some time after it happened that I heard of Mr. Lambert's melancholy death. But it is useless to recur to that painful scene! I resolved to spare no trouble in ascertaining the fate of his daughter. I have only just succeeded, after having almost given her up. I have thought it better to write to you than to her, but I beg you to give her my compliments. I anticipate no difficulty in satisfying you that I am not an impostor. I have no hope of being able to better her circumstances; but, whatever they may be, blood is blood, and cousins are cousins, especially in the West. A speedy answer will oblige yours truly, GEORGE FENTON.

The letter was dated in New York, from an hotel. Roger felt a certain dismay. It had been from the first a peculiar satisfaction to him that Nora began and ended so distinctly with herself. But here was a hint of indefinite continuity! Here, at last, was an echo of her past. He immediately showed the letter to Nora. As she read it, her face flushed deep with wonder and suppressed relief. She had never heard, she confessed, of her mother's half-sister. The "great affection" between the two ladies must have been anterior to Mrs. Lambert's marriage. Roger's own provisional solution of the problem was that Mrs. Lambert had married so little to the taste of her family as to forfeit all communication with them. If he had obeyed his first impulse, he would have written to his mysterious petitioner that Miss Lambert was sensible of the honour implied in his request, but that never having missed his attentions, it seemed needless that, at this time of day, she should cultivate them. But Nora was interested in Mr. Fenton; the dormant pulse of kinship had been quickened; it began to throb with delicious power. This was enough for Roger. "I don't know," he said, "whether he's an honest man or a scamp, but at a venture I suppose

I must invite him down." To this Nora replied that she thought his letter was "so beautiful"; and Mr. Fenton received a fairly civil summons.

Whether or no he was an honest man remained to be seen; but on the face of the matter he appeared no scamp. He was, in fact, a person difficult to classify. Roger had made up his mind that he would be outrageously rough and Western; full of strange oaths and bearded, for aught he knew, like the pard. In aspect, however, Fenton was a pretty fellow enough, and his speech, if not especially conciliatory to ears polite, possessed a certain homely vigour in which ears polite might have found their account. He was as little as possible, certainly, of Roger's circle; but he carried about him the native fragrance of another circle, beside which the social perfume familiar to Roger's nostrils might have seemed a trifle stale and insipid. He was invested with a loose-fitting cosmopolitan Occidentalism, which seemed to say to Roger that, of the two, *he* was the provincial. Considering his years,—they numbered but twenty-five,—Frenton's tough maturity was very wonderful. You would have confessed, however, that he had a true genius for his part, and that it became him better to play at manhood than at juvenility. He could never have been a ruddy-cheeked boy. He was tall and lean, with a keen dark eye, a smile humorous, but not exactly genial, a thin, drawling, almost feminine voice, and a strange South-western accent. His voice, at first, might have given you certain presumptuous hopes as to a soft spot in his stiff young hide; but after listening awhile to its colourless monotone, you would have felt, I think, that though it was an instrument of one string that solitary chord was not likely to become relaxed. Fenton was furthermore flat-chested and high-shouldered, though he was evidently very strong. His straight black hair was always carefully combed, and a small diamond pin adorned the bosom of his shirt. His feet were small and slender, and his left hand was decorated with a neat specimen of tattooing. You never would have called him modest, yet you would hardly have called him impudent; for he had evidently lived with people who had not analysed appreciation to this fine point. He had nothing whatever of the manner of society, but it was surprising how gracefully a certain shrewd *bonhomie* and smart good-humour enabled him to dispense with it. He stood with his hands in his pockets, watching punctilio take its course, and thinking, probably, what a d——d fool she was to go so far roundabout to a point he could reach with a single shuffle of his long legs. Roger, from the first hour of his being in the house, felt pledged to dislike him. Fenton patronised him; he made him feel like a small boy, like an old woman; he sapped the roots of the poor fellow's comfortable consciousness of being a man of the world. Fenton was a man of twenty worlds. He had knocked about and dabbled in affairs and adventures since he was ten years old; he knew the American continent as he knew the palm of his hand; he was redolent of enterprise, of "operations," of a certain fierce friction with mankind. Roger would have liked to believe that he doubted his word, that there was a chance of his not being Nora's cousin, but a youth of an ardent swindling

79

genius who had come into possession of a parcel of facts too provokingly pertinent to be wasted. He had evidently known the late Mr. Lambert,—the poor man must have had plenty of such friends; but was he, in truth, his wife's nephew? Had not this shadowy nepotism been excogitated over an unpaid hotel bill? So Roger fretfully meditated, but generally with no great gain of ground. He inclined, on the whole, to believe the young man's pretensions were valid and to reserve his pugnacity for the use he might possibly make of them. Of course Fenton had not come down to spend a stupid week in the country out of cousinly affection. Nora was but the means; Roger's presumptive wealth and bounty were the end. "He comes to make love to his cousin, and marry her if he can. I, who have done so much, will of course do more; settle an income directly on the bride, make my will in her favour, and die at my earliest convenience! How furious he must be," Roger continued to meditate, "to find me so young and hearty! How furious he would be if he knew a little more!" This line of argument was justified in a manner by the frankness of Fenton's intimation that he was incapable of any other relation to a fact than a desire to turn it to pecuniary account. Roger was uneasy, yet he took a certain comfort in the belief that, thanks to his early lessons, Nora could be trusted to confine her cousin to the limits of cousinship. In whatever he might have failed, he had certainly taught her to know a gentleman. Cousins are born, not made; but lovers may be accepted at discretion. Nora's discretion, surely, would not be wanting. I may add also that, in his desire to order all things well, Roger caught himself wondering whether, at the worst, a little precursory love-making would do any harm. The ground might be gently tickled to receive his own sowing; the petals of the young girl's nature, playfully forced apart, would leave the golden heart of the flower but the more accessible to his own vertical rays.

It was cousinship for Nora, certainly; but cousinship was much; more than Roger fancied, luckily for his peace of mind. To a girl who had never had anything to boast of, this late-coming kinsman seemed a sort of godsend. Nora was so proud of turning out to have a cousin as well as other people, that she treated Fenton much better than other people treat their cousins. It must be said that Fenton was not altogether unworthy of her favours. He meant no especial harm to his fellow-men save in so far as he meant uncompromising benefit to himself. The Knight of La Mancha, on the torrid flats of Spain, never urged his gaunt steed with a grimmer pressure of the knees than that with which Fenton held himself erect on the hungry hobby of success. Shrewd as he was, he had perhaps, as well, a ray of Don Quixote's divine obliquity of vision. It is at least true that success as yet had been painfully elusive, and a part of the peril to Nora's girlish heart lay in this melancholy grace of undeserved failure. The young man's imagination was eager; he had a generous need of keeping too many irons on the fire. His invention was feeling rather jaded when he made overtures to Roger. He had learned six months before of his cousin's situation, and had felt no great sentimental need of making her acquaintance; but at last, revolving many things of a certain sort, he had come to wonder whether these lucky mortals could not be induced to play into his hands. Roger's wealth (which he largely overestimated) and Roger's obvious taste for sharing it with other people, Nora's innocence and Nora's prospects, —it would surely take a great fool not to pluck the rose from so thornless a tree. He foresaw these good things melting and trickling into the empty channel of his own fortune. Exactly what use he meant to make of Nora he would have been at a loss to say. Plain matrimony might or might not be a prize. At any rate, it could do a clever man no harm to have a rich girl foolishly in love with him. He turned, therefore, upon his charming cousin the softer side of his genius. He very soon began to see that he had never known so delightful a person, and indeed his growing sense of her sweetness bade fair to make him bungle his dishonesty. She was altogether sweet enough to be valued for herself. She represented something that he had never yet encountered. Nora was a young lady; how she had come to it was one of the outer mysteries; but there she was, consummate! He made no point of a man being a gentleman; in fact, when a man was a gentleman you had rather to be one yourself, which didn't pay; but for a woman to be a lady was plainly pure gain. He had wit enough to detect something extremely grateful in Nora's half-concessions, her reserve of fresh-ness. Women, to him, had seemed mostly as cut flowers, blooming awhile in the waters of occasion, but yielding no second or rarer satisfaction. Nora was expanding in the sunshine of her cousin's gallantry. She had known so few young men that she had not learned to be fastidious, and Fenton represented to her fancy that great collective manhood from which Roger was excluded by his very virtues. He had an irresistible air of action, alertness, and purpose. Poor Roger held one much less in suspense. She regarded her cousin with something of the thrilled attention which one bestows on the naked arrow, poised across the bow. He had, moreover, the inestimable merit of representing her own side of her situation. He very soon became sensible of this merit, and you may be sure he entertained her to the top of her bent. He gossiped by the hour about her father, and gave her very plainly to understand that poor Mr. Lambert had been more sinned against than sinning.

Nora was not slow to perceive that Roger had no love for their guest, and she immediately conceded him his right of judgement, thinking it natural that they should quarrel about her a little. Fenton's presence was a tacit infringement of Roger's prescriptive right of property. If her cousin had only never come! This might have been, though she could not bring herself to wish it. Nora felt vaguely that here was a chance for tact, for the woman's peace-making art. To keep Roger in spirits, she put on a dozen unwonted graces; she waited on him, appealed to him, smiled at him with unwearied iteration. But the main effect of these sweet offices was to make her cousin think her the prettier. Roger's rancorous suspicion transmuted to bitterness what would otherwise have been pure delight. She was turning hypocrite; she was throwing dust in his eyes; she was plotting with that vulgar Missourian. Fenton, of course, was forced to admit that he had reckoned without his host. Roger had had the impudence not to turn out a simpleton; he was not a shepherd of the golden age; he was a dogged modern, with prosy prejudices; the wind of his favour blew as it listed. Fenton took the liberty of being extremely irritated at the other's want of ductility. "Hang the man!" he said to himself, "why can't he trust me? What is he afraid of? Why don't he take me as a friend rather than an enemy? Let him be frank, and I will be frank. I could put him up to several things. And what does he want to do with Nora, any way?" This latter question Fenton came very soon to answer, and the answer amused him not a little. It seemed to him an extremely odd use of one's time and capital, this fashioning of a wife to order. There was a long-winded patience about it, an arrogance of leisure, which excited his ire. Roger might surely have found *his* fit ready made! His disappointment, a certain angry impulse to break a window, as it were, in Roger's hot-house, the sense finally that what he should gain he would gain from Nora alone, though indeed she was too confoundedly innocent to appreciate his pressing necessities, —these things combined to heat the young man's humour to the fever-point, and to make him strike more random blows than belonged to plain prudence.

The autumn being well advanced, the warmth of the sun had become very grateful. Nora used to spend much of the morning in strolling about the dismantled garden with her cousin. Roger would stand at the window with his honest face more nearly disfigured by a scowl than ever before. It was the old, old story, to his mind: nothing succeeds with women like just too little deference. Fenton would lounge along by Nora's side, with his hands in his pockets, a cigar in his mouth, his shoulders raised to his ears, and a pair of tattered slippers on his absurdly diminutive feet. Not only had Nora forgiven him this last breach of decency, but she had forthwith begun to work him a new pair of slippers. "What on earth," thought Roger, "do they find to talk about?" Their conversation, meanwhile, ran in some such strain as this.

"My dear Nora," said the young man, "what on earth, week in and week out, do you and Mr. Lawrence find to talk about?"

"A great many things, George. We have lived long enough together to have a great many subjects of conversation."

"It was a most extraordinary thing, his adopting you, if you don't mind my saying so. Imagine my adopting a little girl."

"You and Roger are very different men."

"We certainly are. What in the world did he expect to do with you?"

"Very much what he has done, I suppose. He has educated me, he has made me what I am."

"You're a very nice little person; but, upon my word, I don't see that he's to thank for it. A lovely girl can be neither made nor marred."

"Possibly! But I give you notice that I am not a lovely girl. I have it in me to be, under provocation, anything but a lovely girl. I owe everything to Roger. You must say nothing against him. I will not allow it. What would have become of me——" She stopped, betrayed by her glance and voice.

"Mr. Lawrence is a model of all the virtues, I admit! But, Nora, I confess I am jealous of him. Does he expect to educate you for ever? You seem to me to have already all the learning a pretty woman needs. What does *he* know about women? What does he expect to do with you two or three years hence? Two or three years hence you will be number one." And Fenton began to whistle with vehement gaiety, executing with shuffling feet a momentary fandango. "Two or three years hence, when you look in the glass, remember I said so!"

"He means to go to Europe one of these days," said Nora irrelevantly.

"One of these days! One would think he expects to keep you for ever. Not if I can help it. And why Europe, in the name of all that's patriotic? Europe be hanged! You ought to come out to your own section of the country, and see your own people. I can introduce you to the best society in St. Louis. I'll tell you what, my dear. You don't know it, but you're a regular Western girl."

A certain foolish gladness in being the creature thus denominated prompted Nora to a gush of momentary laughter, of which Roger, within the window, caught the soundless ripple. "You ought to know, George," she said, "you are Western enough yourself."

"Of course I am. I glory in it. It's the only place for a man of ideas! In the West you can do something!

Round here you're all stuck fast in ten feet of varnish. For yourself, Nora, at bottom you're all right; but superficially you're just a trifle overstarched. But we'll take it out of you! It comes of living with a stiff-necked——"

Nora bent for a moment her lustrous eyes on the young man, as if to recall him to order. "I beg you to understand, once for all," she said, "that I refuse to listen to disrespectful allusions to Roger."

"I'll say it again, just to make you look at me so. If I ever fall in love with you, it will be when you are scolding me. All I have got to do is to attack your papa——"

"He is not my papa. I have had one papa; that's enough. I say it in all respect."

"If he is not your papa, what is he? He is a dog in the manger. He must be either one thing or the other. When you are very little older, you will understand that."

"He may be whatever thing you please. I shall be but one,—his best friend."

Fenton laughed with a kind of fierce hilarity. "You are so innocent, my dear, that one doesn't know where to take you. Do you expect to marry him?"

Nora stopped in the path, with her eyes on her cousin. For a moment he was half confounded by their startled severity and the flush of pain in her cheek. "Marry Roger!" she said, with great gravity.

"Why, he's a man, after all!"

Nora was silent a moment; and then with a certain forced levity, walking on: "I had better wait till I am asked."

"He will ask you! You will see."

"If he does, I shall be surprised."

"You will pretend to be. Women always do."

"He has known me as a child," she continued, heedless of his sarcasm. "I shall always be a child, for him."

"He will like that," said Fenton. "He will like a child of twenty."

Nora, for an instant, was lost in meditation. "As regards marriage," she said at last, quietly, "I will do what Roger wishes."

Fenton lost patience. "Roger be hanged!" he cried. "You are not his slave. You must choose for yourself and act for yourself. You must obey your own heart. You don't know what you are talking about. One of these days your heart will say its say. Then we shall see what becomes of Roger's wishes! If he wants to make what he pleases of you, he should have taken you younger, —or older! Don't tell me seriously that you can ever love (don't play upon words: love, I mean, in the one sense that means anything!) such a solemn little fop as that! Don't protest, my dear girl; I must have my say. I speak in your own interest; I speak, at any rate, from my own heart. I detest the man. I came here perfectly on the square, and he has treated me as if I weren't fit to touch with tongs. I am poor, I have my way to make, I ain't fashionable; but I'm an honest man, for all that, and as good as he, take me altogether. Why can't he show me a moment's frankness? Why can't he take me by the hand, and say, 'Come, young man, I've got capital, and you've got brains; let's pull together a stroke?' Does he think I want to steal his spoons or pick his pocket? Is that hospitality? It's a poor kind."

This passionate outbreak, prompted in about equal measure by baffled ambition and wounded conceit, made sad havoc with Nora's loyalty to her friend. Her sense of natural property in her cousin,—the instinct of free affection alternating more gratefully than she knew with the dim consciousness of measured dependence,—had become in her heart a sort of sweet excitement. It made her feel that Roger's mistrust was cruel; it was doubly cruel that George should feel it. Two angry men, at any rate, were quarrelling about her, and she must avert an explosion. She promised herself to dismiss Fenton the next day. Of course, by the very fact of this concession, Roger lost ground with her, and George acquired the grace of the persecuted. Meanwhile, Roger's jealous irritation came to a head. On the evening following the little scene I have narrated the young couple sat by the fire in the library; Fenton on a stool at his cousin's feet holding, while Nora wound them on reels, the wools which were to be applied to the manufacture of those invidious slippers. Roger, after grimly watching their mutual amenities for some time over the cover of a book, unable to master his fierce discomposure, departed with a tell-tale stride. They heard him afterwards walking up and down the piazza, where he was appealing from his troubled nerves to the ordered quietude of the stars.

"He hates me so," said Fenton, "that I believe if I were to go out there he would draw a knife."

"O George!" cried Nora, horrified.

89

"It's a fact, my dear. I am afraid you'll have to give me up. I wish I had never seen you!"

"At all events, we can write to each other."

"What's writing? I don't know how to write! I will, though! I suppose he will open my letters. So much the worse for him!"

Nora, as she wound her wool, mused intently. "I can't believe he really grudges me our friendship. It must be something else."

Fenton, with a clench of his fist, arrested suddenly the outflow of the skein from his hand. "It is something else," he said. "It's our possible—more than friendship!" And he grasped her two hands in his own. "Nora, choose! Between me and him!"

She stared a moment; then her eyes filled with tears. "O George," she cried, "you make me very unhappy." She must certainly tell him to go; and yet that very movement of his which had made it doubly needful made it doubly hard. "I will talk to Roger," she said. "No one should be condemned unheard. We may all misunderstand each other."

Fenton, half an hour later, having, as he said, letters to write, went up to his own room; shortly after which, Roger returned to the library. Half an hour's communion with the starlight and the singing crickets had drawn the sting from his irritation. There came to him, too, a mortifying sense of his guest having outdone him in civility. This would never do. He took refuge in imperturbable good-humour, and entered the room in high indifference. But even before he had spoken, something in Nora's face caused this wholesome dose of resignation to stick in his throat. "Your cousin is gone?" he said.

"To his own room. He has some letters to write."

"Shall I hold your wools?" Roger asked, after a pause.

"Thank you. They are all wound."

"For whom are your slippers?" He knew, of course; but the question came.

"For George. Did I not tell you? Do you think them pretty?" And she held up her work.

"Prettier than he deserves."

Nora gave him a rapid glance and miscounted her stitch. "You don't like poor George," she said.

"No. Since you ask me, I don't like poor George."

Nora was silent. At last: "Well!" she said, "you've not the same reasons as I have."

"So I am bound to believe! You must have excellent reasons."

"Excellent. He is my own, you know."

"Your own——? Ah!" And he gave a little laugh.

"My own cousin," said Nora.

"Your own grandfather!" cried Roger.

She stopped her work. "What do you mean?" she asked gravely.

Roger began to blush a little. "I mean—I mean—that I don't believe in your cousin. He doesn't satisfy me. I don't like him. He contradicts himself, his story doesn't hang together. I have nothing but his word. I am not bound to take it."

"Roger, Roger," said Nora, with great softness, "do you mean that he is an impostor?"

"The word is your own. He's not an honest man."

She slowly rose from her little bench, gathering her work into the skirt of her dress. "And, doubting of his honesty, you have let him take up his abode here, you have let him become dear to me?"

She was making him ten times a fool! "Why, if you liked him," he said. "When did I ever refuse you anything?"

There came upon Nora a sudden unpitying sense that Roger was ridiculous. "Honest or not honest," she said with vehemence, "I *do* like him. Cousin or no cousin, he is my friend."

"Very good. But I warn you. I don't enjoy talking to you thus. Only let me tell you, once for all, that your cousin, your friend—your—whatever he is!——" He faltered an instant; Nora's eyes were fixed on him. "That he disgusts me!"

"You are extremely unjust. You have taken no trouble to know him. You have treated him from the first with small civility!"

"Was the trouble to be all mine? Civility! he never missed it; he doesn't know what it means."

"He knows more than you think. But we must talk no more about him." She rolled together her canvas and reels; and then suddenly, with passionate inconsequence, "Poor, poor George!" she cried.

Roger watched her a moment; then he said bitterly, "You disappoint me."

"You must have formed great hopes of me!" she answered.

"I confess I had."

"Say good-bye to them then, Roger. If this is wrong, I am all wrong!" She spoke with a proud decision, which was very becoming; she had never yet come so near being beautiful. In the midst of his passionate vexation, Roger admired her. The scene seemed for a moment a bad dream, from which with a start, he might wake up to tell her he loved her.

"Your anger gives an admirable point to your remarks. Indeed, it gives a beauty to your face. Must a young lady be in the wrong to be attractive?" he went on, hardly knowing what he said. But a burning blush in her cheeks recalled him to a kind of self-abhorrence. "Would to God," he cried, "your abominable cousin had never come between us!"

"Between us? He is not between us. I stand as near you, Roger, as I ever did. Of course George will go away immediately."

"Of course! I am not so sure. He will, I suppose, if he is asked."

"Of course I shall ask him."

"Nonsense. You will not enjoy that."

"We are old friends by this time," said Nora, with terrible irony. "I shall not in the least mind."

Roger could have choked himself. He had brought his case to this: Fenton a martyred proscript, and Nora a brooding victim of duty. "Do I want to turn the man out of the house?" he cried. "Do me a favour—I insist upon it. Say nothing to him, let him stay as long as he chooses. I am not afraid! I don't trust him, but I trust you.

I am curious to see how long he will have the impudence to stay. A fortnight hence I shall be justified. You will say to me, 'Roger, you were right. George is not a gentleman.' There! I insist."

"A gentleman? Really, what are we talking about? Do you mean that he wears a false diamond in his shirt? He will take it off if I ask him. There's a long way between wearing false diamonds——"

"And stealing real ones! I don't know. I have always fancied they go together. At all events, Nora, he is not to suspect that he has been able to make trouble between two old friends."

Nora stood for a moment in irresponsive meditation. "I think he means to go," she said. "If you want him to stay, you must ask him." And without further words, she marched out of the room. Roger followed her with his eyes. He thought of Lady Castlewood in *Henry Esmond*, who looked "devilish handsome in a passion."

Lady Castlewood, meanwhile, ascended to her own room, flung her work upon the floor, and, dropping into a chair, betook herself to weeping. It was late before she slept. She awoke with a new consciousness of the burden of life. Her own burden certainly was small, but her strength, as yet, was untested. She had thought, in her many reveries, of a possible disagreement with Roger, and prayed that it might never come by a fault of hers. The fault was hers now in that she had surely cared less for duty than for joy. Roger, indeed, had shown a pitiful smallness of view. This was a weakness; but who was she, to keep account of Roger's weaknesses? It was to a weakness of Roger's that she owed her food and raiment and shelter. It helped to quench her resentment that she felt, somehow, that, whether Roger smiled or frowned, George would still be George. He was not a gentleman: well and good; neither was she, for that matter, a lady. But a certain manful hardness like George's would not be amiss in the man one was to love.

A simpler soul than Fenton's might have guessed at the trouble of this quiet household. Fenton read in it as well an omen of needful departure. He accepted the necessity with an acute sense of failure,—almost of injury. He had gained nothing but the bother of being loved. It was a bother, because it gave him an unwonted sense of responsibility. It seemed to fling upon all things a dusky shade of prohibition. Yet the matter had its brightness, too, if a man could but swallow his superstitions. He cared for Nora quite enough to tell her he loved her; he had said as much with an easy conscience, to girls for whom he cared far less. He felt gratefully enough the cool vestment of tenderness which she had spun about him, like a web of imponderable silver; but he had other uses for his time than to go masquerading through Nora's fancy. The defeat of his hope that Roger, like a testy old uncle in a comedy, would shower blessings and bank-notes upon his union with his cousin, involved the discomfiture of a secondary project; the design, namely, of borrowing five thousand dollars. The reader will smile; but such is the simplicity of "smart men." He would content himself now with five hundred. In this collapse of his visions he fell a-musing upon Nora's financial value.

"Look here," he said to her, with an air of heroic effort, "I see I'm in the way. I must be off."

"I am sorry, George," said Nora, sadly.

"So am I. I never supposed I was proud. But I reckoned without my host!" he said with a bitter laugh. "I wish I had never come. Or rather I don't. It is worth it all to know you."

She began to question him soothingly about his projects and prospects; and hereupon, for once, Fenton bent his mettle to simulate a pathetic incapacity. He set forth that he was discouraged; the future was a blank. It was child's play, attempting to do anything without capital.

"And you have no capital?" said Nora, anxiously.

Fenton gave a poignant smile. "Why, my dear girl, I'm a poor man!"

"How poor?"

"Poor, poor, poor. Poor as a rat."

"You don't mean that you are penniless?"

"What is the use of my telling you? You can't help me. And it would only make you unhappy."

"If you are unhappy, I want to be!"

This golden vein of sentiment might certainly be worked. Fenton took out his pocket-book, drew from it four bank-notes of five dollars each, and ranged them with a sort of mournful playfulness in a line on his knee. "That's my fortune."

"Do you mean to say that twenty dollars is all you have in the world?"

Fenton smoothed out the creases, caressingly, in the soiled and crumpled notes. "It's a great shame to bring you down to a poor man's secrets," he said. "Fortune has raised you above them."

Nora's heart began to beat. "Yes, it has. I have a little money, George. Some eighty dollars."

Eighty dollars! George suppressed a groan. "He keeps you rather low."

"Why, I have very little use for money, and no chance, here in the country, to spend it. Roger is extremely generous. Every few weeks he makes me take some. I often give it away to the poor people hereabouts. Only a fortnight ago I refused to take any more on account of my still having this. It's agreed between us that I may give what I please in charity, and that my charities are my own affair. If I had only known of you, George, I should have appointed you my pensioner-in-chief."

George was silent. He was wondering intently how he might arrange to become the standing recipient of her overflow. Suddenly he remembered that he ought to protest. But Nora had lightly quitted the room. Fenton repocketed his twenty dollars and awaited her reappearance. Eighty dollars were not a fortune; still they were eighty dollars. To his great annoyance, before Nora returned Roger presented himself. The young man felt for an instant as if he had been caught in an act of sentimental burglary, and made a movement to conciliate his detector. "I am afraid I must bid you good-bye," he said.

Roger frowned, and wondered whether Nora had spoken. At this moment she reappeared, flushed and out of breath with the excitement of her purpose. She had been counting over her money, and held in each hand a little fluttering package of bank-notes. On seeing Roger she stopped and blushed, exchanging with her cousin a rapid glance of inquiry. He almost glared at her, whether with warning or with menace she hardly knew. Roger stood looking at her, half amazed. Suddenly, as the meaning of her errand flashed upon him, he turned a furious crimson. He made a step forward, but cautioned himself; then, folding his arms, he silently waited. Nora, after a moment's hesitation, rolling her notes together, came up to her cousin and held out the little package. Fenton kept his hands in his pockets and devoured her with his eyes. "What's all this?" he said brutally.

"O George!" cried Nora; and her eyes filled with tears.

Roger had divined the situation; the shabby victimisation of the young girl and her kinsman's fury at the disclosure of his avidity. He was angry; but he was even more disgusted. From so vulgar a knave there was little rivalship to fear. "I am afraid I am rather a marplot," he said. "Don't insist, Nora. Wait till my back is turned."

"I have nothing to be ashamed of," said Nora.

"*You?* O, nothing whatever!" cried Roger with a laugh.

Fenton stood leaning against the mantelpiece, desperately sullen, with a look of vicious confusion. "It is only I who have anything to be ashamed of," he said at last, bitterly, with an effort. "My poverty!"

Roger smiled graciously. "Honest poverty is never shameful!"

98

Fenton gave him an insolent stare. "Honest poverty! You know a great deal about it."

"Don't appeal to poor little Nora, man, for her savings," Roger went on. "Come to me."

"You are unjust," said Nora. "He didn't appeal to me. I appealed to him. I guessed his poverty. He has only twenty dollars in the world."

"O you poor little fool!" roared Fenton's eyes.

Roger was delighted. At a single stroke he might redeem his incivility and reinstate himself in Nora's affections. He took out his pocket-book. "Let me help you. It was very stupid of me not to have guessed your embarrassment." And he counted out a dozen notes.

Nora stepped to her cousin's side and passed her hand through his arm. "Don't be proud," she murmured caressingly.

Roger's notes were new and crisp. Fenton looked hard at the opposite wall, but, explain it who can, he read their successive figures,—a fifty, four twenties, six tens. He could have howled.

"Come, don't be proud," repeated Roger, holding out this little bundle of wealth.

Two great passionate tears welled into the young man's eyes. The sight of Roger's sturdy sleekness, of the comfortable twinkle of patronage in his eye, was too much for him. "I shall not give *you* a chance to be proud," he said. "Take care! Your papers may go into the fire."

"O George!" murmured Nora; and her murmur seemed to him delicious.

He bent down his head, passed his arm round her

shoulders, and kissed her on her forehead. "Good-bye, dearest Nora," he said.

Roger stood staring, with his proffered gift. "You decline?" he cried, almost defiantly.

"'Decline' is not the word. A man does not decline an insult."

Was Fenton, then, to have the best of it, and was his own very generosity to be turned against him? Blindly, passionately, Roger crumpled the notes into his fist and tossed them into the fire. In an instant they began to blaze.

"Roger, are you mad?" cried Nora. And she made a movement to rescue the crackling paper. Fenton burst into a laugh. He caught her by the arm, clasped her round the waist, and forced her to stand and watch the brief blaze. Pressed against his side, she felt the quick beating of his heart. As the notes disappeared her eyes sought Roger's face. He looked at her stupidly, and then turning on his heel he walked out of the room. Her cousin, still holding her, showered upon her forehead half-a-dozen fierce kisses. But disengaging herself—"You must leave the house!" she cried. "Something dreadful will happen."

Fenton had soon packed his valise, and Nora, meanwhile, had ordered a vehicle to carry him to the station. She waited for him in the portico. When he came out with his bag in his hand, she offered him again her little roll of bills. But he was a wiser man than half an hour before. He took them, turned them over, and selected a one-dollar note. "I will keep this," he said, "in remembrance, and only spend it for my last dinner." She made him promise, however, that if trouble really overtook him, he would let her know, and in any case he would write. As the wagon went over the crest of an adjoining hill he stood up and waved his hat. His tall, gaunt young figure, as it rose dark against the cold November sunset, cast a cooling shadow across the fount of her virgin sympathies. Such was the outline, surely, of the conquering hero, not of the conquered. Her fancy followed him forth into the world with a sense of comradeship.

V

ROGER'S quarrel with his young companion, if quarrel it was, was never repaired. It had scattered its seed; they were left lying, to be absorbed in the conscious soil or dispersed by some benignant breeze of accident, as destiny might appoint. But as a manner of clearing the air of its thunder, Roger, a week after Fenton's departure, proposed she should go with him for a fortnight to town. Later, perhaps, they might arrange to remain for the winter. Nora had been longing vaguely for the relief of a change of circumstances; she assented with great good-will. They lodged at an hotel,—not the establishment at which they had made acquaintance. Here, late in the afternoon, the day after their arrival, Nora sat by the window, waiting for Roger to come and take her to dinner, and watching with the intentness of country eyes the hurrying throng in the street; thinking too at moments of a certain blue bonnet she had bought that morning, and comparing it, not uncomplacently, with the transitory bonnets on the pavement. A gentleman was introduced; Nora had not forgotten Hubert Lawrence. Hubert had occupied for more than a year past a pastoral office in the West, and had recently had little communication with his cousin. Nora he had seen but on a single occasion, that of his visit to Roger, six months after her advent. She had grown in the interval, from the little girl who slept with *The Child's Own Book* under her pillow and dreamed of the Prince Avenant, into a lofty maiden who reperused *The Heir of Redclyffe*, and mused upon the loves of the clergy. Hubert, too, had changed in his own degree. He was now thirty-one years of age, and his character had lost something of a certain boyish vagueness of outline, which formerly had not been without its grace. But his elder grace was scarcely less effective. Various possible half-shadows in his personality had melted into broad, shallow lights. He was now, distinctly, one of the light-armed troops of the army of the Lord. He fought the Devil as an irresponsible skirmisher, not as a sturdy gunsman planted beside a booming sixty-pounder. The clerical cloth, as Hubert wore it, was not unmitigated sable; and in spite of his cloth, such as it was, humanity rather than divinity got the lion's share of his attentions. He loved doubtless, in this world, the heavenward face of things, but he loved, as regards heaven, the earthward. He was rather an idler in the walks of theology, and he was uncommitted to any very rigid convictions. He thought the old theological positions in very bad taste, but he thought the new theological negations in no taste at all. In fact, Hubert believed so vaguely and languidly in the Devil that there was but slender logic in his having undertaken the cure of souls. He administered his spiritual medicines in homœpathic doses. It had been maliciously said that he had turned parson because parsons enjoy peculiar advantages in approaching the fair sex. The presumption is in their favour. Our business, however, is not to pick up idle reports. Hubert was, on the whole, a decidedly light weight, and yet his want of spiritual passion was by no means, in effect, a want of motive or stimulus; for the central pivot of his being continued to operate with the most noiseless precision and regularity, —the slim, erect, inflexible *Ego*. To the eyes of men, and especially to the eyes of woman, whatever may have been the moving cause, the outer manifestation was very agreeable. If Hubert had no great firmness of faith, he had a very pretty firmness of manner. He was gentle without timidity, frank without arrogance, clever without pedantry. The common measure of clerical disallowance was reduced in his hands to the tacit protest of a generous personal purity. His appearance bore various wholesome traces of the practical lessons of his Western pastorate. This had not been to his taste; he had had to apply himself, to devote himself, to compromise with a hundred aversions. His talents had been worth less to him than he expected, and he had been obliged, as the French say, to *payer de sa personne*,—that person for which he entertained so delicate a respect. All this had given him a slightly jaded, overwearied look, certain to deepen his interest in feminine eyes. He had actually a couple of fine wrinkles in his seraphic forehead. He secretly rejoiced in his wrinkles. They were his crown of glory. He had suffered, he had worked, he had been bored. Now he believed in earthly compensations.

"Dear me!" he said, "can this be Nora Lambert?"

She had risen to meet him, and held out her hand with girlish frankness. She was dressed in a light silk dress; she seemed a young woman grown. "I have been growing hard in all these years," she said. "I have had to catch up with

104

those *pieds énormes*." The readers will not have forgotten that Hubert had thus qualified her lower members. Ignorant as she was, at the moment, of the French tongue, her memory had instinctively retained the words, and she had taken an early opportunity to look out *pied* in the dictionary. *Énorme*, of course, spoke for itself.

"You must have caught up with them now," Hubert said, laughing. "You are an enormous young lady. I should never have known you." He sat down, asked various questions about Roger, and adjured her to tell him, as he said, "all about herself." The invitation was flattering, but it met only a partial compliance. Unconscious as yet of her own charm, Nora was oppressed by a secret admiration of her companion, whose presence seemed to open a brilliant vista. She compared him with her cousin, and wondered that he should be at once so impressive and so different. She blushed a little, privately, for Fenton, and was not ill pleased to think he was absent. In the light of Hubert's good manners, his admission that he was no gentleman acquired an excessive force. By this thrilling intimation of the diversity of the male sex, the mental pinafore of childhood seemed finally dismissed. Hubert was so frank and friendly, so tenderly and gallantly patronising, that more than once she felt herself beginning to expand; but then, suddenly, something absent in the tone of his assent, a vague fancy that, in the gathering dusk, he was looking at her all at his ease, rather than listening to her, converted her bravery into what she knew to be deplorable little-girlishness. On the whole, this interview may have passed for Nora's first lesson in the art, indispensable to a young lady on the threshold of society, of talking for half an hour without saying anything. The lesson was interrupted by the arrival of Roger, who greeted his cousin with almost extravagant warmth, and insisted upon his staying to dinner. Roger was to take Nora after dinner to a concert, for which he felt no great enthusiasm; he proposed to Hubert, who was a musical man, to occupy his place. Hubert demurred awhile; but in the meantime Nora, having gone to prepare herself, reappeared, looking extremely well in the blue crape bonnet before mentioned, with her face bright with anticipated pleasure. For a moment Roger was vexed at having resigned his office; Hubert immediately stepped into it. They came home late, the blue bonnet nothing the worse for wear, and the young girl's face lighted up by her impressions. Her animation was extreme; she treated Roger to a representation of the concert, and made a great show of voice. Her departing childishness, her dawning tact, her freedom with Roger, her half-freedom with Hubert, made a charming mixture, and insured for her auditors the success of the entertainment. When she had retired, amid a mimic storm of applause from the two gentlemen, Roger solemnly addressed his cousin. "Well, what do you think of her? I hope you have no fault to find with her feet."

"I have had no observation of her feet," said Hubert; "but she will have very handsome hands. She is a very nice creature." Roger sat lounging in his chair with his hands in his pockets, his chin on his breast, and a heavy gaze fixed on Hubert. The latter was struck with his deeply preoccupied aspect. "But let us talk of you rather than of Nora," he said. "I have been waiting for a chance to tell you that you look very poorly."

"Nora or I,—it's all one. She is the only thing in life I care for."

Hubert was startled by the sombre energy of his tone. The old polished, placid Roger was in abeyance. "My dear fellow," he said, "you are altogether wrong. Live for yourself. You may be sure she will do as much. You take it too hard."

"Yes, I take it too hard. It troubles me."

"What's the matter? Is she a naughty child? Is she more than you bargained for?" Roger sat gazing at him in silence, with the same grave eye. He began to suspect Nora had turned out a losing investment. "Has she—a —low tastes?" he went on. "Surely not with that sweet face!"

Roger started to his feet impatiently. "Don't misunderstand me!" he cried. "I have been longing to see some one,—to talk—to get some advice,—some sympathy. I am fretting myself away."

"Good heavens, man, give her a thousand dollars and send her back to her family. You have educated her."

"Her family! She has no family! She's the loneliest as well as the sweetest, wisest, best of creatures! If she were only a tenth as good, I should be a happier man. I can't think of parting with her; not for all I possess."

Hubert stared a moment. "Why, you are in love."

"Yes," said Roger, blushing. "I am in love."

"Dear me!" murmured Hubert.

"I am not ashamed of it," rejoined Roger, softly.

It was no business of Hubert's certainly; but he felt the least bit disappointed. "Well," he said coolly, "why don't you marry her?"

"It is not so simple as that!"

"She will not have you?"

Roger frowned impatiently. "Reflect a moment. You pretend to be a man of delicacy."

"You mean she is too young? Nonsense. If you are sure of her, the younger the better."

"For my unutterable misery," said Roger, "I have a conscience. I wish to leave her free and take the risk. I wish to be just and let the matter work itself out. You may think me absurd, but I wish to be loved for myself, as other men are loved."

It was a specialty of Hubert's that in proportion as other people grew hot, he grew cool. To keep cool, morally, in a heated medium was, in fact, for Hubert a peculiar satisfaction. He broke into a long light laugh. "Excuse me," he said, "but there is something ludicrous in your attitude. What business has a lover with a conscience? None at all! That's why I keep out of it. It seems to me your prerogative to be downright. If you waste any more time in hair-splitting, you will find your young lady has taken things in the lump!"

"Do you really think there is danger?" Roger demanded, pitifully. "Not yet awhile. She's only a child.

Tell me, rather, *is* she only a child? You have spent the evening beside her: how does she strike a stranger?"

While Hubert's answer lingered on his lips, the door opened and Nora came in. Her errand was to demand the use of Roger's watch-key, her own having mysteriously vanished. She had begun to take out her pins and had muffled herself for this excursion in a merino dressing-gown of sombre blue. Her hair was gathered for the night into a single massive coil, which had been loosened by the rapidity of her flight along the passage. Roger's key proved a complete misfit, so that she had recourse to Hubert's. It hung on the watch-chain which depended from his waistcoat, and some rather intimate fumbling was needed to adjust it to Nora's diminutive timepiece. It worked admirably, and she stood looking at him with a little smile of caution as it creaked on the pivot. "I would not have troubled you," she said, "but that without my watch I should oversleep myself. You know Roger's temper, and what I should suffer if I were late for breakfast!"

Roger was ravished at this humorous sally, and when, on making her escape, she clasped one hand to her head to support her released tresses, and hurried along the corridor with the other confining the skirts of her inflated robe, he kissed his hand after her with more than jocular good-will.

"Ah! it's as bad as that!" said Hubert, shaking his head.

"I had no idea she had such hair," murmured Roger. "You are right, it is no case for shilly-shallying."

"Take care!" said Hubert. "She is only a child."

Roger looked at him a moment. "My dear fellow, you are a hypocrite."

Hubert coloured the least bit, and then took up his hat and began to smooth it with his handkerchief. "Not at all. See how frank I can be. I recommend you to marry the young lady and have done with it. If you wait, it will be at your own risk. I assure you I think she is charming, and if I am not mistaken, this is only a hint of future possibilities. Don't sow for others to reap. If you think the harvest is not ripe, let it ripen in milder sun-beams than these vigorous hand-kisses. Lodge her with some proper person and go to Europe; come home from Paris a year hence with her trousseau in your trunks, and I will perform the ceremony without another fee than the prospect of having an adorable cousin." With these words Hubert left his companion pensive.

His words reverberated in Roger's mind; I may almost say that they rankled. A couple of days later, in the hope of tenderer counsel, he called upon our friend Mrs. Keith. This lady had completely rounded the cape of matri-mony, and was now buoyantly at anchor in the placid cove of well-dowered widowhood. You have heard many a young unmarried lady exclaim with a bold sweep of con-ception, "Ah me! I wish I were a widow!" Mrs. Keith was precisely the widow that young unmarried ladies wish to be. With her diamonds in her dressing-case and her carriage in her stable, and without a feather's weight of encumbrance, she offered a finished example of satis-fied ambition. Her wants had been definite; these once gratified, she had not presumed further. She was a very much worthier woman than in those hungry virginal days when Roger had wooed her. Prosperity had agreed equally well with her beauty and her temper. The wrinkles on her brow had stood still, like Joshua's sun, and a host of good intentions and fair promises seemed to illuminate her person. Roger, as he stood before her, not only felt that his passion was incurably defunct, but allowed himself to doubt that this *veuve consolée* would have made an ideal wife. The lady mistaking his embarrassment for the fumes of smouldering ardour, determined to transmute his devotion by the subtle chemistry of friendship. This she found easy work; in ten minutes the echoes of the past were hushed in the small-talk of the present. Mrs. Keith was on the point of sailing for Europe, and had much to say of her plans and arrangements,—of the miserable rent she was to get for her house. "Why shouldn't one turn an honest penny?" she asked. "And now," she went on, when the field had been cleared, "tell me about the young lady." This was precisely what Roger wished; but just as he was about to begin his story there came an irruption of visitors, fatal to the confidential. Mrs. Keith found means to take him aside. "Seeing is better than hearing," she said, "and I am dying to see her. Bring her this evening to dinner, and we shall have her to ourselves."

Mrs. Keith had long been for Nora an object of mystical veneration. Roger had been in the habit of alluding to her, not freely nor frequently, but with a certain implicit consideration which more than once had set Nora wondering. She entered the lady's drawing-room that evening

with an oppressive desire to please. The interest manifested by Roger in the question of what she should wear
assured her that he had staked a nameless something on
the impression she might make. She was not only reassured, however, but altogether captivated, by the lavish
cordiality of her hostess. Mrs. Keith kissed her on both
cheeks, held her at her two arms' length, gave a twist to the
fall of her sash, and made her feel very plainly that she
was being inspected and appraised. All this was done,
however, with a certain flattering light in the eye and a
tender matronly smile which rather increased than diminished the young girl's composure. Mrs. Keith was herself
so elegant, so finished, so fragrant of taste and sense, that
before an hour was over Nora felt that she had borrowed
the hint of a dozen indispensable graces. After dinner her
hostess bade her sit down to the piano. Here, feeling sure
of her ground, Nora surpassed herself. Mrs. Keith
beckoned to Roger to come and sit beside her on the sofa,
where, as she nodded time to the music with her head,
she softly conversed. Prosperity, as I have intimated,
had acted on her moral nature very much as a medicinal
tonic—quinine or iron—acts upon the physical. She was
in a comfortable glow of charity. She itched gently, she
hardly knew where,—was it in heart or brain?—to
render some one a service. She had on hand a small capital
of sentimental patronage for which she desired a secure
investment. Here was her chance. The project which
Roger had imparted to her three years before seemed to
her, now she had taken Nora's measure, to contain such
pretty elements of success that she deemed it a sovereign

pity it should not be rounded into symmetry. She determined to lend an artistic hand. "Does she know it, that matter?" she asked in a whisper.

"I have never told her."

"That's right. I approve your delicacy. Of course you are sure of your case. She is altogether lovely,—she is one in a thousand. I really envy you; upon my word, Mr. Lawrence, I am jealous. She has a style of her own. It is not quite beauty; it is not quite cleverness. It belongs neither altogether to her person, nor yet to her mind. It's a kind of way she has. It's a way that may lead her far. She has pretty things, too; one of these days she may take it into her head to be a beauty of beauties. Nature never meant her to hold up her head so well for nothing. Ah, how wrinkled and faded it makes one feel! To be sixteen years old, with that head of hair, with health and good connections, with that amount of good-will at the piano, it's the very best thing in the world, if they but knew it! But no! they must leave it all behind them; they must pull their hair to pieces; they must get rid of their complexions; they must be twenty; they must have lovers, and go their own gait. Well, since it must come, we must attend to the profits: they will take care of the pleasures. Give Nora to me for a year. She needs a woman, a wise woman, a woman like me. Men, when they undertake to meddle with a young girl's education, are veriest old grandmothers. Let me take her to Europe and bring her out in Rome. Don't be afraid; I will guard your interests. I will bring you back the most charming girl in America. I see her from here!" And describing a great curve in the air with her fan, Mrs. Keith inclined her head to one side in a manner suggestive of a milliner who descries in the bosom of futurity the ideal bonnet. Looking at Roger, she saw that her point was gained; and Nora, having just finished her piece, was accordingly summoned to the sofa and made to sit down at Mrs. Keith's feet. Roger went and stood before the fire. "My dear Nora," said Mrs. Keith, as if she had known her from childhood, "how should you like to go with me to Rome?"

Nora started to her feet, and stood looking open-eyed from one to the other. "Really?" she said. "Does Roger——"

"Roger," said Mrs. Keith, "finds you so hard to manage that he has made you over to me. I forewarn you, I am a terrible woman. But if you are not afraid, I shall scold you and pinch you no harder than I would a daughter of my own."

"I give you up for a year," said Roger. "It is hard, troublesome as you are."

Nora stood wavering for a moment, hesitating where to deposit her excess of joy. Then graciously dropping on her knees before Mrs. Keith, she bent her young head and got rid of it in an ample kiss. "I am not afraid of you," she said simply. Roger turned round and began to poke the fire.

The next day Nora went forth to buy certain articles necessary in travelling. It was raining so heavily that, at Roger's direction, she took a carriage. Coming out of a shop, in the course of her expedition, she encountered

Hubert Lawrence tramping along in the wet. He helped her back to her carriage, and stood for a moment talking to her through the window. As they were going in the same direction, she invited him to get in; and on his hesitating, she added that she hoped their interview was not to end there, as she was going to Europe with Mrs. Keith. At this news Hubert jumped in and placed himself on the front seat. The knowledge that she was drifting away gave a sudden value to the present occasion. Add to this that in the light of Roger's revelation after the concert, this passive, predestined figure of hers had acquired for the young man a certain picturesque interest. Nora found herself strangely at ease with her companion. From time to time she strove to check her happy freedom: but Hubert evidently, with his superior urbanity, was not the person to note a little more or less in a school-girl's primness. Her enjoyment of his presence, her elation in the prospect of departure, made her gaiety reckless. They went together to half-a-dozen shops and talked and laughed so distractedly over her purchases, that she made them sadly at haphazard. At last their progress was arrested by a dead-lock of vehicles in front of them, caused by the breaking down of a street-car. The carriage drew up near the sidewalk in front of a confectioner's. On Nora's regretting the delay, and saying she was ravenous for lunch, Hubert went into the shop, and returned with a bundle of tarts. The rain came down in sheeted torrents, so that they had to close both the windows. Circled about with this watery screen, they feasted on their tarts with peculiar relish. In a short time

Hubert made another excursion, and returned with a second course. His diving to and fro in the rain excited them to extravagant mirth. Nora had bought some pocket-handkerchiefs, which were in that cohesive state common to these articles in the shop. It seemed a very pretty joke to spread the piece across their knees as a table-cloth.

"To think of picnicking in the midst of Washington Street!" cried Nora, with her lips besprinkled with flakes of pastry.

"For a young lady about to leave her native land, her home, and friends, and all that is dear to her," said Hubert, "you seem to me in very good spirits."

"Don't speak of it," said Nora. "I shall cry to-night; it is feverish gaiety."

"You will not be able to do this kind of thing abroad," said Hubert. "Do you know we are monstrously improper? For a young girl it's by no means pure gain, going to Europe. She comes into a very pretty heritage of prohibitions. You have no idea of the number of improper things a young girl can do. You are walking on the edge of a precipice. Don't look over or you will lose your head and never walk straight again. Here, you are all blindfold. Promise me not to lose this blessed bandage of American innocence. Promise me that, when you come back, we shall spend another morning together as free and delightful as this one!"

"I promise you!" said Nora; but Hubert's words had potently foreshadowed the forfeiture of sweet possibilities. For the rest of the drive she was in a graver mood.

They found Roger beneath the portico of the hotel, watch in hand, staring up and down the street. Preceding events having been explained to him, he offered to drive his cousin home.

"I suppose Nora has told you," he began, as they proceeded.

"Yes! Well, I am sorry. She is a charming girl."

"Ah!" Roger cried; "I knew you thought so!"

"You are as knowing as ever! She sails, she tells me, on Wednesday next. And you, when do you sail?"

"I don't sail at all. I am going home."

"Are you sure of that?"

Roger gazed for a moment out of the window. "I mean for a year," he said, "to allow her perfect liberty."

"And to accept the consequences?"

"Absolutely." And Roger folded his arms.

This conversation took place on a Friday. Nora was to sail from New York on the succeeding Wednesday; for which purpose she was to leave Boston with Mrs. Keith on the Monday. The two ladies were of course to be attended to the ship by Roger. Early Sunday morning Nora received a visit from her friend. The reader will perhaps remember that Mrs. Keith was a recent convert to the Roman Catholic faith; as such, she performed her religious duties with peculiar assiduity. Her present errand was to propose that Nora should go with her to church and join in offering a mass for their safety at sea. "I don't want to bring you over, you know; but I think it would be so nice," said Mrs. Keith. Appealing to Roger, Nora received permission to do as she chose; she therefore lent herself with fervour to this pious enterprise. The two ladies spent an hour at the foot of the altar,—an hour of romantic delight to the younger one. On Sunday evening Roger, who, as the day of separation approached, became painfully anxious and reluctant, betook himself to Mrs. Keith, with the desire to enforce upon her mind a solemn sense of her responsibilities and of the value of the treasure he had confided to her. Nora, left alone, sat wondering whether Hubert might not come to bid her farewell. Wandering listlessly about the room, her eye fell on the Saturday evening paper. She took it up and glanced down the columns. In one of them she perceived a list of the various church services of the morrow. Last in the line stood this announcement: "At the —— —— Church, the Rev. Hubert Lawrence, at eight o'clock." It gave her a gentle shock; it destroyed the vision of his coming in and their having, under the lamp, by the fire, the serious counterpart of their frolicsome *tête-à-tête* in the carriage. She longed to show him that she was not a giggling child, but a wise young lady. But no; in a dimly-crowded church, before a hundred eyes, he was speaking of divine things. How did he look in the pulpit? If she could only see him! And why not? She looked at her watch; it lacked ten minutes to eight. She made no pause to reflect; she only felt that she must hurry. She rang the bell and ordered a carriage, and then, hastening to her room, put on her shawl and bonnet,—the blue crape bonnet of the concert. In a few moments she was on her way to the church. When she reached it, her heart was beating fast; she was on the point of turning back. But the coachman opened the carriage door with such a flourish that she was ashamed not to get out. She was late; the church was full, the service had gone forward, the sermon was about to begin. The sexton with great solemnity conducted her up the aisle to a pew directly beneath the pulpit. She bent her eyes on the ground, but she knew that there was a deep expectant silence, and that Hubert was upright before the desk looking at her. She sat down beside a very grim-visaged old lady with bushy eyebrows, who stared at her so hard, that to hide her confusion she buried her head and prolonged her prayer; upon which the old lady seemed to stare more intently, as if she thought her very pretentious. When she raised her head, Hubert had begun to speak; he was looking above her and beyond her, and during the sermon his level glance never met her own. Of what did he speak and what was the moral of his discourse? Nora could not have told you; yet not a soul in the audience, not all those listening souls together, were more devoutly attentive than she. But it was not on what he said, but on what he was, or seemed to be, that her perception was centred. Hubert Lawrence had an excellent gift of oratory. His voice was full of penetrating sweetness, and, modulated with infinite art, it sank with a silvery cadence. His speech was silver, though I doubt whether his silence was ever golden. His utterance seemed to Nora the perfection of eloquence. She thought of her uplifted feeling in the morning, in the incense-thickened air of the Catholic church; but what a straighter flight to heaven was this! Hubert's week-day face was a summer cloud, with a lining of celestial brightness. Now, how the divine truth over-lapped its relenting edges and seemed to transform it into a dazzling focus of light! He spoke for half an hour, but Nora took no note of time. As the service drew to a close, he gave her from the pulpit a rapid glance, which she interpreted as a request to remain. When the congrega-tion began to disperse, a number of persons, chiefly ladies, waited for him near the pulpit, and, as he came down, met him with greetings and compliments. Nora watched him from her place, listening, smiling, and pass-ing his handkerchief over his forehead. At last they re-leased him, and he came up to her. She remembered for years afterward the strange half-smile on his face. There was something in it like a pair of eyes peeping over a wall. It seemed to express so fine an acquiescence in what she had done, that, for the moment, she had a startled sense of having committed herself to something. He gave her his hand, without manifesting any surprise. "How did you get here?"

"In a carriage. I saw it in the paper at the last moment."

"Does Roger know you came?"

"No; he had gone to Mrs. Keith's."

"So you started off alone, at a moment's notice?"

She nodded, blushing. He was still holding her hand; he pressed it and dropped it. "O Hubert," cried Nora suddenly, "*now* I know you!"

Two ladies were lingering near, apparently mother and daughter. "I must be civil to them," he said; "they have come from New York to hear me." He quickly rejoined them and conducted them toward their carriage. The younger one was extremely pretty, and looked a little like a Jewess. Nora observed that she wore a great diamond in each ear; she eyed our heroine rather severely as they passed. In a few minutes Hubert came back, and, before she knew it, she had taken his arm and he was beside her in her own carriage. They drove to the hotel in silence; he went upstairs with her. Roger had not returned. "Mrs. Keith is very agreeable," said Hubert. "But Roger knew that long ago. I suppose you have heard," he added; "but perhaps you have not heard."

"I have not heard," said Nora, "but I have suspected——"

"What?"

"No; it is for you to say."

"Why, that Mrs. Keith might have been Mrs. Lawrence."

"Ah, I was right,—I was right," murmured Nora, with a little air of triumph. "She may be still. I wish she would!" Nora was removing her bonnet before the mirror over the chimney-piece; as she spoke, she caught Hubert's eye in the glass. He dropped it and took up his hat. "Won't you wait?" she asked.

He said he thought he had better go, but he lingered without sitting down. Nora walked about the room, she hardly knew why, smoothing the table-covers and rearranging the chairs.

"Did you cry about your departure, the other night, as you promised?" Hubert asked.

"I confess that I was so tired with our adventures that I went straight to sleep."

"Keep your tears for a better cause. One of the greatest pleasures in life is in store for you. There are a hundred things I should like to say to you about Rome. How I only wish I were going to show it you! Let me beg you to go some day to a little place in the Via Felice, on the Pincian,—a house with a terrace adjoining the fourth floor. There is a plasterer's shop in the basement. You can reach the terrace by the common staircase. I occupied the rooms adjoining it, and it was my peculiar property. I remember I used often to share it with a poor little American sculptress who lived below. She made my bust; the Apollo Belvedere was nothing to it. I wonder what has become of her! Take a look at the view,—the view I woke up to every morning, read by, studied by, lived by. I used to alternate my periods of sight-seeing with fits of passionate study. In another winter I think I might have learned something. Your real lover of Rome oscillates with a kind of delicious pain between the city in itself and the city in literature, They keep for ever referring you to each other and bandying you to and fro. If we had eyes for metaphysical things, Nora, you might see a hundred odd bits of old ambitions and day-dreams strewing that little terrace. Ah, as I sat there, how the Campagna used to take up the tale and respond to my printed page! If I know anything of the lesson of history (a man of my profession is supposed to), I learned it in that enchanted air! I should like to know who is sitting in the same school now. Perhaps you will write me a word."

"I will piously gather up the crumbs of your feasts and

make a meal of them," said Nora. "I will let you know how they taste."

"Pray do. And one more request. Don't let Mrs. Keith make a Catholic of you." And he put out his hand.

She shook her head slowly, as she took it. "I will have no Pope but you," she said.

And after that he went.

VI

ROGER had assured his cousin that he meant to return home, and indeed, after Nora's departure, he spent a fortnight in the country. But finding he had no patience left for solitude, he again came to town and established himself for the winter. A restless need of getting rid of time caused him to resume his earlier social habits. It began to be said of him that now he had disposed of that queer little girl that he had picked up Heaven knew where (whom it was certainly very good-natured of Mrs. Keith to take off his hands), he was going to look about him for a young person whom he might take to his home in earnest. Roger felt as if he were now establishing himself in society in behalf of that larger personality into which his narrow singleness was destined to expand. He was paving the way for Nora. It seemed to him that she might find it an easy way to tread. He compared her attentively with every young girl he met; many were prettier, some possessed in larger degree the air of "brightness"; but none revealed that deep-shrined natural force, lurking in the shadow of modesty like a statue in a recess, which you hardly know whether to denominate humility or pride.

One evening, at a large party, Roger found himself approached by an elderly lady who had known him from his boyhood and for whom he had a traditional regard, but with whom of late years he had relaxed his intercourse, from a feeling that, being a very worldly old woman, her influence on Nora might be pernicious. She had never smiled on the episode of which Nora was the heroine, and she hailed Roger's reappearance as a sign that this episode was at an end and that he had repented of his abrupt eccentricity. She was somewhat cynical in her shrewdness, and so far as she might, she handled matters without gloves.

"I am glad to see you have found your wits again," she said, "and that that forlorn little orphan—Dora, Flora, what's her name?—has not altogether made a fool of you. You want to marry; come, don't deny it. You can no more remain unmarried than I can remain standing here. Go ask that little man for his chair. With your means and your disposition and all the rest of it, you ought by this time to be setting a good example. But it's never too late to mend. I have got the thing for you. Have you been introduced to Miss Sands? Who is Miss Sands? There you are to the life! Miss Sands is Miss Sands, the young lady in whose honour we are here convened. She is staying with my sister. You must have heard of her. New York, but good New York; so pretty that she might be as silly as you please, yet as clever and good as if she were as plain as I. She is everything a man can want. If you have not seen her it's providential. Come; don't protest for the sake of protesting. I have thought it all out. Allow me! in this matter I am a woman of genius. I know at a glance what will do and what won't. You are made for each other. Come and be presented. You have just time to settle down to it before supper."

Then came into Roger's honest visage a sort of Mephis-
tophelian glee,—the momentary intoxication of duplicity.
"Well, well," he said, "let us see all that's to be seen."
And he thought of his Peruvian Teresa. Miss Sands,
however, proved no Teresa, and Roger's friend had not
overstated her merits. Her beauty was remarkable; and
strangely, in spite of her blooming maturity, something
in her expression, her smile, reminded him forcibly of
Nora. So Nora might look after ten or twelve years of
evening parties. There was a hint, just a hint, of custo-
mary triumph in the poise of her head, an air of serene
success in her carriage; but it was her especial charm that
she seemed to melt downward and condescend from this
altitude of loveliness with a benignant and considerate
grace; to drop, as it were, from the zenith of her favour,
with a little shake of invitation, the silken cable of a
gradual smile. Roger felt that there was so little to be
feared from her that he actually enjoyed the mere surface-
glow of his admiration; the sense of floating unmelted in
the genial zone of her presence, like a polar ice-block in a
summer sea. The more he observed her, the more she
seemed to foreshadow his prospective Nora; so that at
last, borrowing confidence from this phantasmal identity,
he addressed her with unaffected friendliness. Miss Sands,
who was a woman of perceptions, seeing an obviously
modest man swimming, as it were, in this mystical calm,
became interested. She divined in Roger's manner an
unusual species of admiration. She had feasted her fill on
uttered flattery; but here was a good man whose appreciation left compliments far behind. At the end of ten

minutes Roger mentioned that she reminded him singularly of a young girl he knew. "A young girl, forsooth," thought Miss Sands. "Is he coming to his *fadaises*, like the rest of them?"

"You are older than she," Roger added, "but I expect her to look like you some time hence."

"I gladly bequeath her my youth, as I come to give it up."

"You can never have been plain," said Roger. "My friend, just now, is no beauty. But I assure you, you encourage me."

"Tell me about this young lady," his companion rejoined. "It is interesting to hear about people one looks like."

"I should like to tell you," said Roger, "but you would laugh at me."

"You do me injustice. Evidently this is a matter of sentiment. Genuine sentiment is the best thing in the world; and when I catch myself laughing at a mortal who confesses to it, I submit to being told that I have grown old only to grow silly."

Roger smiled approval. "I can only say," he answered, "that this young friend of mine is, to me, the most interesting object in the world."

"In other words, you are engaged to marry her."

"Not a bit of it."

"Why, then, she is a deaf-mute whom you have rendered vocal, or a pretty heathen whom you have brought to Sunday school."

Roger laughed exuberantly. "You have hit it," he

said; "a deaf-mute whom I have taught to speak. Add to that, that she was a little blind, and that now she recognises me with spectacles, and you will admit that I have reason to be proud of my work." Then, after a pause he pursued, seriously, "If anything were to happen to her——"

"If she were to lose her faculties——"

"I should be in despair. But I know what I should do. I should come to you."

"O, I should be a poor substitute!"

"I should make love to you," Roger went on.

"You would be in despair indeed. But you must bring me some supper."

Half an hour later, as the ladies were cloaking themselves, Mrs. Middleton, who had undertaken Roger's case, asked Miss Sands for her impressions. These seemed to have been highly propitious. "He is not a shining light, perhaps," the young lady said, "but he is an honest man. He is in earnest; after what I have been through, that is very pleasant. And by the way, what is this little deaf and dumb girl in whom he is interested?"

Mrs. Middleton stared. "I never heard she was deaf and dumb. Very likely. He adopted her and brought her up. He has sent her abroad—to learn the languages!"

Miss Sands mused as they descended the stairs. "He is a good man," she said. "I like him."

It was in consequence, doubtless, of this last remark that Roger, the next morning, received a note from his friend. "You have made a hit; I shall never forgive you if you don't follow it up. You have only to be decently civil and then propose. Come and dine with me on Wednesday. I shall have only one guest. You know I always take a nap after dinner."

The same post that brought Mrs. Middleton's note brought a letter from Nora. It was dated from Rome, and ran as follows:—

"I hardly know, dearest Roger, whether to begin with an apology or a scolding. We have each something to forgive, but you have certainly least. I have before me your two poor little notes, which I have been reading over for the twentieth time; trying, in this city of miracles, to work upon them the miracle of the loaves and fishes. But the miracle won't come: they remain only two very much bethumbed epistles. Dear Roger, I have been extremely vexed and uneasy. I have fancied you were ill, or, worse, —that out of sight is out of mind. It is not with me, I assure you. I have written you *twelve* little letters. They have been short only because I have been horribly busy. To-day I declined an invitation to drive on the Campagna, on purpose to write to you. The Campagna,— do you hear? I can hardly believe that, five months ago, I was watching the ripe apples drop in the orchard at C——. We are always on our second floor on the Pincian, with plenty of sun, which you know is the great necessity here. Close at hand are the great steps of the Piazza di Spagna, where the beggars and models sit at the receipt of custom. Some of them are so handsome, sunning themselves there in their picturesqueness, that I cannot help wishing I knew how to paint or draw. I wish I had been a good girl three years ago and done as you wished, and taken drawing-lessons in earnest. Dear Roger, I never neglected your advice but to my cost. Mrs. Keith is extremely kind, and determined I shall have not come abroad to 'mope,' as she says. She does not care much for sight-seeing, having done it all before; though she keeps pretty well *au courant* of the various church festivals. She very often talks of you, and is very fond of you. She is full of good points, but that is her best one. My own sight-seeing habits do not at all incommode her, owing to my having made the acquaintance of a little old German lady who lives at the top of our house. She is a queer wizened oddity of a woman, but she is very clever and friendly, and she has the things of Rome on her fingers' ends. The reason of her being here is very sad and beautiful. Twelve years ago her younger sister, a beautiful girl (she has shown me her miniature), was deceived and abandoned by her betrothed. She fled away from her home, and after many weary wanderings found her way to Rome, and gained admission to the convent with the dreadful name,—the Sepolte Vive. Here, ever since, she has been immured. The inmates are literally buried alive; they are dead to the outer world. My poor little Mademoiselle Stamm followed her and took up her dwelling here, to be near her. But they have a dead stone wall between them. For twelve years she has never seen her. Her only communication with Lisa—her conventual name she doesn't even know—is once a week to deposit a bouquet of flowers, with her name attached, in the little blind wicket of the convent wall. To do this with her own hands, she lives in Rome. She composes her bouquet with a kind of passion; I have seen her and helped her. Fortunately flowers in Rome are very cheap, for my friend is deplorably poor. I have had a little pleasure, or rather a great pleasure. For the past two months I have furnished the flowers, and I assure you we have had the best. I go each time with Mademoiselle Stamm to the wicket, and we put in our bouquet and see it gobbled up into the speechless maw of the cloister. It is a dismal amusement, but I confess it interests me. I feel as if I knew this poor Lisa; though, after all, she may be dead, and we may be worshipping a shadow. But in this city of shadows and memories, what is one shadow the more? Don't think, however, that we spend all our time in playing with shadows. We go everywhere, we see everything; I could not be in better hands. Mrs. Keith has doubts about my friend's moral influence; she accuses her of being a German philosopher in petticoats. She is a German, she wears petticoats; and having known poverty and unhappiness, she is obliged to be something of a philosopher. As for her metaphysics, they may be very wicked, but I should be too stupid to understand them, and it is less trouble to abide by my own— and Mrs. Keith's! At all events, I have told her all about you, and she says you are the one good man she ever heard of; so it's not for you to disapprove of her! My mornings I spend with her; after lunch I go out with Mrs. Keith. We drive to the various villas, make visits upon all kinds of people, go to studios and churches and palaces. In the evenings we hold high revel. Mrs. Keith knows every one; she receives a great many people, and we go out in proportion. It is a most amusing world. I have seen more people in the last six weeks than I ever expected to in a lifetime. I feel so old,—you wouldn't know me! One grows more in a month in this wonderful Rome than in a year at home. Mrs. Keith is very much liked and admired. She has lightened her mourning and looks much better; but, as she says, she will never be herself till she gets back to pink. As for me, I wear pink and blue and every colour of the rainbow. It appears that everything suits me; there is no spoiling me. Of course, I am *out*, —a thousand miles out. I came out six weeks ago at the great ball of the Princess X. How the Princess X.— poor lady!—came to serve my turn, is more than I can say; but Mrs. Keith is a fairy godmother; she shod me in glass slippers and we went. I fortunately came home with my slippers on my feet. I was very much frightened when we went in. I courtesied to the Princess: and the Princess stared good-naturedly; while I heard Mrs. Keith behind me whispering, 'Lower, lower!' But I have yet to learn how to courtesy to condescending princesses. Now I can drop a little bow to a good old cardinal as smartly as you please. Mrs. Keith has presented me to half-a-dozen, with whom I pass, I suppose, for an interesting convert. Alas, I am only a convert to worldly vanities, which I confess I vastly enjoy. Dear Roger, I am hopelessly frivolous. The shrinking diffidence of childhood I have utterly cast away. I speak up at people as bold as brass. I like having them introduced to me, and having to be interested and interesting at a moment's notice. I like listening and watching; I like sitting up to the small hours; I like talking myself. But I need hardly to tell you this, at the end of my ten pages of chatter. I have talked about my own affairs, because I know they will interest you. Profit by my good example, and tell me all about yours. Do you miss me? I have read over and over your two little notes, to find some little hint that you do; but not a word! I confess I wouldn't have you too unhappy. I am so glad to hear you are in town, and not at that dreary, wintry C——. Is our old C—— life at an end, I wonder? Nothing can ever be the same after a winter in Rome. Sometimes I am half frightened at having had it in my youth. It leaves such a chance to be dull afterwards! But I shall come back some day with you. And not even the Princess X. shall make me forget my winter seat by the library fire at C——, my summer seat under the great elm."

This production seemed to Roger a marvel of intellectual promise and epistolary grace; it filled his eyes with grateful tears; he carried it in his pocket-book and read it to a dozen people. His tears, however, were partly those of penitence, as well as of delight. He had had a purpose in preserving that silence, which had cost so much to his good-nature. He wished to make Nora miss him, and to let silence combine with absence to plead for him. Had he succeeded? Not too well, it would seem; yet well enough to make him feel that he had been cruel. His letter occupied him so intensely that it was not till within an hour of Mrs. Middleton's dinner that he remembered his engagement. In the drawing-room he found Miss Sands, looking even more beautiful in a dark high-necked dress

133

than in the glory of gauze and flowers. During dinner he was in excellent spirits; he uttered perhaps no epigrams, but he gave, by his laughter, an epigrammatic turn to the ladyish gossip of his companions. Mrs. Middleton entertained the best hopes. When they had left the table she betook herself to her arm-chair, and erected a little handscreen before her face, behind which she slept or not, as you choose. Roger, suddenly bethinking himself that if Miss Sands had been made a party to the old lady's views, his alacrity of manner might compromise him, checked his vivacity, and asked his companion stiffly if she played the piano. On her confessing to this accomplishment, he of course proceeded to open the instrument which stood in the adjoining room. Here Miss Sands sat down and played with great resolution an exquisite composition of Schubert. As she struck the last note he uttered some superlative of praise. She was silent for a moment, and then, "That is a thing I rarely play," she said.

"It is very difficult, I suppose."

"It is not only difficult, but it is too sad."

"Sad!" cried Roger, "I should call it very joyous."

"You must be in very good spirits! I take it to have been meant for pure sadness. This is what should suit your mood!" and she attacked with great animation one of Strauss's waltzes. But she had played but a dozen chords when he interrupted her. "Spare me," he said. "I may be glad, but not with that gladness. I confess that I *am* in spirits. I have just had a letter from that young friend of whom I spoke to you."

"Your adopted daughter? Mrs. Middleton told me about her."

"Mrs. Middleton," said Roger, in downright fashion, "knows nothing about her. Mrs. Middleton," and he lowered his voice and laughed, "is not an oracle of wisdom." He glanced into the other room at their hostess and her complaisant screen. He felt with peculiar intensity that, whether she was napping or no, she was a sadly superficial—in fact a positively immoral—old woman. It seemed absurd to believe that this fair, wise creature before him had lent herself to a scheme of such a one's making. He looked awhile at her deep clear eyes and her gracious lips. It would be a satisfaction to smile with her over Mrs. Middleton's machinations. "Do you know what she wants to do with us?" he went on. "She wants to make a match between us."

He waited for her smile, but it was heralded by a blush, —a blush portentous, formidable, tragical. Like a sudden glow of sunset in a noonday sky, it covered her fair face and burned on her cloudless brow. "The deuce!" thought Roger. "Can it be,—can it be?" The smile he had invoked followed fast; but this was not the order of nature.

"A match between *us*!" said Miss Sands. "What a brilliant idea!"

"Not that I cannot easily imagine falling in love with you," Roger rejoined; "but—but——"

"But you are in love with some one else." Her eyes, for a moment, rested on him intently. "With your protégée!"

135

Roger hesitated. It seemed odd to be making this sacred confidence to a stranger; but with this matter of Mrs. Middleton's little arrangement between them, she was hardly a stranger. If he had offended her, too, the part of gallantry was to admit everything. "Yes, I am in love!" he said. "And with the young lady you so much resemble. She doesn't know it. Only one or two persons know it, save yourself. It is the secret of my life, Miss Sands. She is abroad. I have wished to do what I could for her. It is an odd sort of position, you know. I have brought her up with the view of making her my wife, but I have never breathed a word of it to her. She must choose for herself. My hope is that she will choose me. But Heaven knows what turn she may take, what may happen to her over there in Rome. I hope for the best; but I think of little else. Meanwhile I go about with a sober face, and eat and sleep and talk, like the rest of the world; but all the while I am counting the hours. Really, I don't know what has set me going in this way. I don't suppose you will at all understand my situation; but you are evidently so good that I feel as if I might count on your sympathy."

Miss Sands listened with her eyes bent downward and with great gravity. When he had spoken, she gave him her hand with a certain passionate abruptness. "You have my sympathy!" she said. "Much good may it do you! I know nothing of your friend, but it is hard to fancy her disappointing you. I perhaps don't altogether enter into your situation. It is novel, but it is extremely interesting. I hope before rejecting you she will think twice. I don't bestow my esteem at random, but you have it, Mr.

Lawrence, absolutely." And with these words she rose. At the same moment their hostess suspended her siesta, and the conversation became general. It can hardly be said, however, to have prospered. Miss Sands talked with a certain gracious zeal which was not unallied, I imagine, to a desire to efface the trace of that superb blush I have attempted to chronicle. Roger brooded and wondered; and Mrs. Middleton, fancying that things were not going well, expressed her displeasure by abusing every one who was mentioned. She took heart again for the moment when, on the young lady's carriage being announced, the latter, turning in farewell to Roger, asked him if he ever came to New York. "When you are next there," she said, "you must make a point of coming to see me. You will have something to tell me."

After she had gone Roger demanded of Mrs. Middleton whether she had imparted to Miss Sands her scheme for their common felicity. "Never mind what I said or did not say," she replied. "She knows enough not to be taken unawares. And now tell me——" But Roger would tell her nothing. He made his escape, and as he walked home in the frosty starlight, his face wore a smile of the most shameless elation. He had gone up in the market. Nora might do worse! There stood that beautiful woman knocking at his door.

A few evenings after this Roger called upon Hubert. Not immediately, but on what may be called the second line of conversation, Hubert asked him what news he had from Nora. Roger replied by reading her letter aloud. For some moments after he had finished Hubert was silent. "'One grows more in a month in this wonderful Rome,'" he said at last, quoting, "'than in a year at home.'"

"Grow, grow, grow, and Heaven speed it!" said Roger.

"She is growing, you may depend upon it."

"Of course she is; and yet," said Roger, discriminatingly, "there is a kind of girlish freshness, a childish simplicity, in her style."

"Strongly marked," said Hubert, laughing. "I have just got a letter from her you would take to be written by a child of ten."

"*You* have a letter?"

"It came an hour ago. Let me read it."

"Had you written to her?"

"Not a word. But you will see." And Hubert in his dressing-gown, standing before the fire, with the same silver-sounding accents Nora had admired, distilled her own gentle prose into Roger's attentive ear.

"I have not forgotten your asking me to write to you about your beloved Pincian view. Indeed, I have been daily reminded of it by having that same view continually before my eyes. From my own window I see the same dark Rome, the same blue Campagna. I have rigorously performed my promise, however, of ascending to your little terrace. I have an old German friend here, a perfect archaeologist in petticoats, in whose company I think as little of climbing to terraces and towers as of diving into catacombs and crypts. We chose the finest day of the winter, and made the pilgrimage together. The plaster-merchant is still in the basement. We saw him in his doorway, standing to dry, whitened over as if he meant personally to be cast. We reached your terrace in safety. It was flooded with light,—you know the Roman light, —the yellow and the purple. A young painter who occupies your rooms had set up his easel under an umbrella in the open air. A young *contadina*, imported, I suppose, from the Piazza di Spagna, was sitting to him in the sunshine, which deepened her brown face, her blue-black hair, and her white head-cloth. He was flattering her to his heart's content, and of course to hers. When I want my portrait painted, I shall know where to go. My friend explained to him that we had come to look at his terrace on behalf of an unhappy far-away American gentleman who had once been lodger there. Hereupon he was charmingly polite. He showed us the little *salotto*, the fragment of bas-relief inserted in the wall,—was it there in your day?—and a dozen of his own pictures. One of them was a very pretty version of the view from the terrace. Does it betray an indecent greed for applause to let you know that I bought it, and that, if you are very good and write me a delightful long letter, you shall have it when I get home? It seemed to me that you would be glad to learn that your little habitation is not turned to baser uses, and that genius and ambition may still be found there. In your case, I suppose, they were not found in company with dark-eyed *contadine*, though they had an admirer in the person of that poor little American sculptress. I asked the young painter if she had left any memory behind her. Only a memory, it appears. She died a month after his arrival. I never was so bountifully thanked for anything as for buying our young man's picture. As he poured out his lovely Italian gratitude, I felt like some patronising duchess of the Renaissance. You will have to do your best, when I transfer the picture to your hands, to give as pretty a turn to your thanks. This is only one specimen of a hundred delightful rambles I have had with Mlle. Stamm. We go a great deal to the churches; I never tire of them. Not in the least that I am turning Papist, though in Mrs. Keith's society, if I chose to do so, I might treat myself to the luxury of being a nine days' wonder (admire my self-denial!), but because they are so picturesque and historic; so redolent of memories, so rich with traditions, so haunted with the past. To go into most of the churches is like reading some novel, better than I find most novels. They are for different days. On a fine day, if I have on my best bonnet, if I have been to a party the night before, I like to go to Santa-Maria Maggiore. Standing there, I dream, I dream, I dream; I should be ashamed to tell you the nonsense I *do* dream! On a rainy day, when I tramp out with Mlle. Stamm in my waterproof; when the evening before, instead of going to a party, I have sat quietly at home reading Rio's *Art Chrétien* (recommended by the Abbé Leblond, Mrs. Keith's confessor), I like to go to the Ara Cœli. There you stand among the very bric-à-brac of Christian history. Something takes you at the throat,—but you will have felt it; I needn't try to define the indefinable. Nevertheless, in spite of M. Rio and the Abbé Leblond (he is a very charming old man too, and a keeper of *ladies'* consciences, if there ever was one), there is small danger of my changing my present faith for one that will make it a sin to go and hear you preach. Of course, we don't only haunt the churches. I know in a way the Vatican, the Capitol, and those charming galleries of the great palaces. Of course, you know them far better. I am stopped short on every side by my deplorable ignorance; still, as far as may be given to a silly girl, I enjoy. I wish you were here, or that I knew some benevolent man of culture. My little German duenna is a marvel of learning and communicativeness, and when she fairly harangues me, I feel as if in my single person I were a young ladies' boarding-school. But only a man can talk really to the point of this manliest of cities. Mrs. Keith sees a great many gentlemen of one sort and another; but what do they know of Brutus and Augustus, of Emperors and Popes? I shall keep my impressions, such as they are, and we shall talk them over at our leisure. I shall bring home plenty of photographs; we shall have charming evenings looking at them. Roger writes that he means next winter to take a furnished house in town. You must come often and see us. We are to spend the summer in England. . . . Do you often see Roger? I suppose so,—he wrote he was having a 'capital winter.' By the way, I am 'out.' I go to balls and wear Paris dresses. I toil not, neither do I spin. There is apparently no end to my banker's account, and Mrs. Keith sets me a prodigious example of buying. Is Roger meanwhile going about with patched elbows?"

At this point Hubert stopped, and, on Roger's asking

him if there was nothing more, declared that the rest was private. "As you please," said Roger. "By Jove! what a letter,—what a letter!"

Several months later, in September, he hired for the ensuing winter a small furnished house. Mrs. Keith and her companion were expected to reach home on the 10th of October. On the 6th, Roger took possession of his house. Most of the rooms had been repainted, and on preparing to establish himself in one for the night, Roger found that the fresh paint emitted such an odour as to make his position untenable. Exploring the premises, he discovered in the lower regions, in a kind of sub-basement, a small vacant apartment, destined to a servant, in which he had a bed put up. It was damp, but as he thought, not too damp, the basement being dry, as basements go. For three nights he occupied this room. On the fourth morning he woke up with a chill and a headache. By noon he had a fever. The physician, being sent for, pronounced him seriously ill, and assured him that he had been guilty of a gross imprudence. He might as well have slept in a burial-vault. It was the first sanitary indiscretion Roger had ever committed; he had a dismal foreboding of its results. Towards evening the fever deepened, and he began to lose his head. He was still distinctly conscious that Nora was to arrive on the morrow, and sadly disgusted that she was to find him in this sorry plight. It was a bitter disappointment that he might not meet her at the steamer. Still, Hubert might go. He sent for Hubert accordingly, who was brought to his bedside. "I shall be all right in a day or two," he said, "but meanwhile some one must receive Nora. I know you will be glad to do it, you villain!"

Hubert declared that he was no villain, but that he should be happy to perform this service. As he looked at his poor fever-stricken cousin, however, he doubted strongly if Roger would be "all right" in a day or two. On the morrow he went down to the ship.

VII

On arriving at the landing-place of the European steamer, Hubert found the passengers filing ashore from the tug-boat in which they had been transferred from the ship. He instructed himself, as he took his place near the gang-way, to allow for a certain change in Nora's appearance; but even with this allowance none of the various advancing ladies seemed to be Nora. Suddenly he found himself confronted with a fair stranger, a smile, and an outstretched hand. The smile and the offered hand of course proclaimed the young lady's identity. Yet in spite of them, Hubert's surprise was great; his allowance had been too small. But the next moment, "Now you speak," he said, "I recognise you"; and the next he had greeted Mrs. Keith, who immediately followed her companion; after which he ushered the two ladies, with their servant and their various feminine *impedimenta*, into a carriage. Mrs. Keith was to return directly to her own house, where, hospitable even amid prospective chaos, she invited Hubert to join them at dinner. He had, of course, been obliged to inform Nora offhand of the cause of Roger's absence, though as yet he made light of his illness. It was agreed, however, that Nora should remain with her companion until she had communicated with her guardian.

Entering Mrs. Keith's drawing-room a couple of hours later, Hubert found the young girl on her knees before the hearth. He sat down near by, and in the glow of the firelight he noted her altered aspect. A year, somehow, had made more than a year's difference. Hubert, in his intercourse with women, was accustomed to indulge in a sort of cool contemplation which, as a habit, found favour according to the sensibility of the ladies touching whom it was practised. It had been intimated to him more than once, that, in spite of his cloth, just a certain turn of the head made this a license. But on this occasion his gaze was all respectful. He was lost in admiration; for Nora was beautiful. She had left home a simple maiden of common gifts, with no greater burden of loveliness than the slender, angular, neutral grace of youth and freshness; and here she stood, a mature, consummate, superb young woman! It was as if she had bloomed into ripeness in the sunshine of a great contentment; as if, fed by the sources of æsthetic delight, her nature had risen calmly to its allotted level. A singular harmony and serenity seemed to pervade her person. Her beauty lay in no inordinate perfection of individual features, but in the deep sweet fellowship that reigned between smile and step and glance and tone. The total effect was an impression of the simplest and yet the richest loveliness. "Pallas Athene," said Hubert to himself, "sprang full-armed, we are told, from the brain of Jove. But we have a Western version of the myth. She was born in Missouri; for years she wore aprons and carried lesson-books. Then one fine day she was eighteen, and she sported a black silk dress of Paris!" Meanwhile Pallas Athene had been asking about Roger. "Shall I see him to-morrow, at least?" she demanded.

"I think not; he will not get out for several days."

"But I can easily go to him. It is very tiresome. Things never turn out as we arrange them. I had arranged this meeting of ours to perfection! He was to dine with us here, and we were to talk, talk, talk till midnight; and then I was to go home with him; and there we were to stand leaning on the banisters at his room door, and talk, talk, talk till morning."

"And where was I to be?" asked Hubert.

"I had not arranged for you. But I expected to see you to-morrow. To-morrow I shall go to Roger."

"If the doctor allows," said Hubert.

Nora rose to her feet. "You don't mean to say, Hubert, that it is as bad as *that*?" She frowned a little and bent her eyes eagerly on his face. Hubert heard Mrs. Keith's voice in the hall; in a moment their *tête-à-tête* would be at an end. Instead of answering her question,—"Nora," he said, in his deepest, lowest voice, "you are wonderfully beautiful!" He caught her startled, unsatisfied glance; then he turned and greeted Mrs. Keith. He had not pleased Nora, evidently; it was premature. So to efface the solemnity of his speech, he repeated it aloud: "I tell Nora she is very beautiful!"

"Bah!" said Mrs. Keith; "you needn't tell her; she knows it."

Nora smiled unconfusedly. "O, say it all the same!"

"Was it not the French ambassador, in Rome," Mrs. Keith demanded, "who attacked you in that fashion? He asked to be introduced. There's an honour! '*Mademoiselle, vous êtes parfaitement belle.*'"

"He was very ugly himself," said Nora.

Hubert was a lover of the luxuries and splendours of life. He had no immediate personal need of them; he could make his terms with narrow circumstances; but his imagination was a born aristocrat. He liked to be reminded that certain things were,—ambassadors, ambassadorial compliments, Old-World drawing-rooms with duskily moulded ceilings. Nora's beauty, to his vision, took a deeper colour from this homage of an old starched and embroidered diplomatist. It was valid, it had passed the ordeal. He had little need at table to play at discreet inattention. Mrs. Keith, preoccupied with her housekeeping and the "dreadful state" in which her freshly departed tenants had left her rooms, indulged in a tragic monologue and dispensed with responses. Nora, looking frankly at Hubert, consoled their hostess with gentle optimism; and Hubert returned her looks, wondering. He mused upon the mystery of beauty. What sudden magic had made her so handsome? She was the same tender slip of girlhood who had come trembling to hear him preach a year before; the same, yet how different! And how sufficient she had grown, withal, to her beauty! How with the added burden had come an added strength, —with the greater charm a greater force,—a force subtle, sensitive, just faintly self-suspecting. Then came the thought that all this was Roger's,—Roger's speculation. Roger's property! He pitied the poor fellow, lying senseless and helpless instead of sitting there delightedly, drawing her out and showing her off. After dinner Nora talked little, partly, as he felt, from anxiety about her friend, and partly because of that natural reserve of the altered mind when confronted with old associations. He would have been glad to believe that she was taking pensive note of his own appearance. He had made his mark in her mind a twelvemonth before. Innumerable scenes and figures had since passed over it; but his figure, Nora now discovered, had not been obliterated. Fixed there indelibly, it had grown with the growth of her imagination. She knew that she had changed, and she had wondered whether Hubert would have lost favour with difference. Would he suffer by contrast with people she had seen? Would he seem graceless, colourless, common? Little by little, as his presence defined itself, it became plain to her that the Hubert of the past had a lease of the future. As he rose to take his leave, she begged him to let her write a line to Roger, which he might carry.

"He will not be able to read it," said Hubert.

Nora mused. "I will write it, nevertheless. You will place it by his bedside, and the moment he is better he will find it at hand."

When she had left the room, Mrs. Keith demanded tribute. "Have not I done well? Have not I made a charming girl of her?"

"She does you great credit," said Hubert, with a mental reservation.

"O, but wait awhile! You have not seen her yet. She is tired, and anxious about your cousin. Wait till she comes out. My dear Mr. Lawrence, she is perfect. She lacks nothing, she has nothing too much. You must do me justice. I saw it all in the rough, and I knew just what it wanted. I wish she were my daughter: you should see great doings! And she's as good as gold. It's her nature. After all, unless your nature is right, what are you?" But before Hubert could reply to this little philosophic proposition, Nora reappeared with her note.

The next morning Mrs. Keith went to call officially upon her mother-in-law; and Nora left alone, and thinking much of Roger's condition, conceived an intense desire to see him. He had never been so dear to her as now, and no one's right to be with him was equal to hers. She dressed hastily and repaired to the little dwelling they were to have so happily occupied. She was admitted by her old friend Lucinda, who, between trouble and wonder, found a thousand things to say. Nora's beauty had never received warmer tribute than the affectionate marvellings of this old woman who had known her early plainness so well. She led her into the drawing-room, opened the windows and turned her about in the light, patted her braided tresses, and rejoiced with motherly unction in her tallness and straightness and elegance. Of Roger she spoke with tearful eyes. "It would be for him to see you, my dear," she said; "he would not be disappointed. You are better than his brightest dreams. O, I know all about it! He used to talk to me evenings, after you were in bed, 'Lucinda, do you think she's pretty? Lucinda, do you think she's plain? Lucinda, do you dress her warm? Lucinda, have you changed her shoes? And mind, Lucinda, take good care of her hair; it's the only thing we are sure of!' Yes, my dear, you have me to thank for these big braids. Would he feel sure of you now, poor man? You must keep yourself in cotton-wool till he recovers. You are like a picture; you ought to be enclosed in a gilt frame and stand against the wall." Lucinda begged, however, that Nora would not insist upon seeing him; and her great reluctance betraying his evil case, Nora consented to wait. Her own small experience could avail nothing. "He is flighty," said Lucinda, "and I'm afraid he wouldn't recognise you. If he shouldn't, it would do you no good; and if he should, it would do him none; it would increase his fever. He's bad, my dear, he's bad; but leave him to me! I nursed him as a baby; I nursed him as a boy; I will nurse him as a man grown. I have seen him worse than this, with the scarlet fever at college, when his poor mother was dying at home. Baby, boy, and man, he has always had the patience of a saint. I will keep him for you, Miss Nora, now I have seen you! I shouldn't dare to meet him in heaven, if I were to let him miss you!"

When Lucinda had returned to her bedside duties, Nora wandered about the house with a soundless tread, taking melancholy note of the preparations Roger had made for her return. His choice, his taste, his ingenuity, were everywhere visible. The best beloved of her possessions from the old house in the country had been transferred hither and placed in such kindly half-lights as would temper justice with mercy; others had found expensive substitutes. Nora went into the drawing-room, where the blinds were closed and the chairs and sofas shrouded in brown linen, and sat sadly revolving possibilities. How, with Roger's death, loneliness again would close about her; how he was her world, her strength, her fate! He had made her life; she needed him still to watch his work. She seemed to apprehend as by a sudden supernatural light, the extent of his affection and his wisdom. In the perfect stillness of the house she could almost hear his tread on the stairs, hear his voice utter her name with that tender adjustment of tone which conveyed a benediction in a commonplace. Her heart rose to her throat; she felt a passionate desire to scream. She buried her head in a cushion to stifle the sound; her silent tears fell upon the silk. Suddenly she heard a step in the hall; she had only time to brush them away before Hubert Lawrence came in. He greeted her with surprise. "I came to bring your note," he said; "I did not expect to find you."

"Where better should I be?" she asked, with intensity. "I can do nothing here, but I should look ill elsewhere. Give me back my note, please. It does not say half I feel." He gave it back, and stood watching her while she tore it in bits and threw it into the empty fireplace. "I have been wandering over the house," she added. "Everything tells me of poor Roger." She felt an indefinable need of protesting of her affection for him. "I never knew till now," she said, "how much I loved him. I am sure you don't know him, Hubert; not as I do. I don't believe any one does. People always speak of him with a little air of amusement. Even Mrs. Keith is witty at his expense. But I know him; I grew to know him in thinking of him while I was away. There is more of him than the world knows or than the world would ever know, if it were left to his modesty and the world's stupidity!" Hubert began to smile at her eloquence. "But I mean to put an end to his modesty. I mean to say, 'Come, Roger, hold up your head and speak out your mind and do yourself justice.' I have seen people without a quarter of his goodness who had twenty times his assurance and his success. I shall turn the tables! People shall have no favour from me, unless they are good to Roger. If they want me, they must take him too. They tell me I am a beauty, and I can do what I please. We shall see. The first thing I shall do will be to make them show him a great deal of respect."

"I admire your spirit," said Hubert. "Dr. Johnson liked a good hater; I like a good lover. On the whole, it's more rarely found. But aren't you the least bit Quixotic, with your terrible loyalty? No one denies that Roger is the best of the best of the best! But do what you please, Nora, you cannot make virtue entertaining. As a clergyman, you know, I have had to try it. But it's no use; there's a fatal family likeness between goodness and dullness. Of course you are fond of Roger. So am I, so is every one in his heart of hearts. But what are we to do about it? The kindest thing is to leave him alone. His virtues are his own affair. You describe him perfectly when you say that everything in the house here sings his praise,— already, before he has been here ten days! The chairs are all straight, the pictures are admirably hung, the locks are oiled, the winter fuel is stocked, the bills are paid! Look at the tidies pinned on the chairs. I will warrant you he pinned them with his own hands. Such is Roger!

Such virtues, in a household, are priceless. He ought never to marry; his wife would die for want of occupation. What society cares for in a man is not his household virtues, but his worldly ones. I am talking now, of course, as a man of the world. Society wants to see things by the large end of the telescope, not by the small. 'Be as good as you please,' it says, 'but unless you are interesting, I'll none of you!'"

"Interesting!" cried Nora, with a rosy flush. "I have seen some very interesting people who have bored me to death. But if people don't care for Roger, it's their own loss!" Pausing a moment she fixed Hubert with the searching candour of her gaze. "You are unjust," she said.

This charge was pleasant to the young man's soul; he would not, for the world, have summarily rebutted it. "Explain, dear cousin," he said, smiling kindly. "Wherein am I unjust?"

It was the first time he had called her cousin; the word made a sweet confusion in her thoughts. But looking at him still while she collected them, "You don't care to know!" she cried. "Not when you smile so! You are laughing at me, at Roger, at every one!" Clever men had ere this been called dreadfully satirical by pretty women; but never, surely, with just that imperious naïveté. She spoke with a kind of joy in her frankness; the sense of intimacy with the young man had effaced the sense of difference.

"The scoffing fiend! That's a pretty character to give a clergyman!" said Hubert.

"Are you, at heart, a clergyman? I have been wondering."

"You have heard me preach."

"Yes, a year ago, when I was a silly little girl. I want to hear you again."

"No, I have gained my crown, I propose to keep it. I would rather not be found out. Besides, I am not preaching now; I am resting. Some people think me a clergyman, Nora," he said, lowering his voice with a hint of mock humility. "But do you know you are formidable, with your fierce friendships and your jealous suspicions? If you doubt of me, well and good. Let me walk like an Homeric god in a cloud; without my cloud, I should be sadly ungodlike. Indeed, for that matter, I doubt of myself. But I don't really undervalue Roger. I love him, I admire him, I envy him. I would give the world to be able to exchange my restless imagination for his silent, sturdy usefulness. I feel as if I were toiling in the sun, and he were sitting under green trees resting from an effort which he has never needed to make. Well, virtue, I suppose, is welcome to the shade. It's cool, but it's dreadfully obscure! People are free to find out the best and the worst of *me*! Here I stand, with all my imperfections on my head; tricked out with a surplice, baptized with a *reverend* (Heaven save the mark!), equipped with platform and pulpit and text and audience,—erected into a mouthpiece of the spiritual aspirations of mankind. Well, I confess our sins; that's good humble-minded work. And I must say, in justice, that when once I don my surplice (I insist on the surplice, I can do nothing without it) and mount into the pulpit, I feel conscious of a certain power. They call it eloquence; I suppose it is. I don't know what it's worth, but they seem to like it."

Nora sat speechless, with expanded eyes, hardly knowing whether his humility or his audacity became him best; flattered, above all, by what she deemed the recklessness of his confidence. She had removed her hat, which she held in her hand, gently curling its great black feather. Few things in a woman could be prettier than her uncovered forehead, illumined with her gentle wonder. The moment, for Hubert, was critical. He knew that a young girl's heart stood trembling on the verge of his influence; he felt, without fatuity, that a glance might beckon her forward, a word might fix her there. Should he speak his word? This mystic circle was haunted with the rustling ghosts of women who had ventured within and found no rest. But as the innermost meaning of Nora's beauty grew vivid before him, it seemed to him that she, at least, might cleanse it of its sinister memories and fill it with the sense of peace. He knew that to such as Nora he was no dispenser of peace; but as he looked at her she seemed to him as an angel knocking at his gates. He could not turn her away. Let her come, at her risk! For angels there is a special providence. "Don't think me worse than I am," he said, "but don't think me better! I shall love Roger well until I begin to fancy that you love him too well. Then,—it's absurd, perhaps, but I feel it will be so,—I shall be jealous."

The words were lightly uttered, but his eyes and voice

gave them meaning. Nora coloured and rose; she went to the mirror and put on her hat. Then turning round with a laugh which, to one in the secret, might have seemed to sound the coming-of-age of her maiden's fancy, "If you mean to be jealous," she said, "now is your time! I love Roger now with all my heart. I cannot do more!" She remained but a moment longer.

Roger's illness baffled the doctors, though the doctors were clever. For a fortnight it went from bad to worse. Nora remained constantly at home, and played but a passive part to the little social drama enacted in Mrs. Keith's drawing-room. This lady had already cleared her stage and rung up her curtain. To the temporary indisposition of her young performer she resigned herself with that serene good grace which she had always at command, and which was so subtle an intermixture of kindness and shrewdness that it would have taken a wiser head than Nora's to discriminate them. She valued the young girl for her social uses; but she spared her at this trying hour, just as an impresario, with an eye to the whole season, spares a prima donna who is threatened with bronchitis. Between these two, though there was little natural sympathy, there was a wondrous exchange of caresses and civilities. They had quietly judged each other and each sat serenely encamped in her estimate as in a strategical position. Nevertheless I would have trusted neither lady's account of the other. Nora, for perfect fairness, had too much to learn, and Mrs. Keith too much to unlearn. With her companion, however, she had unlearned much of that circumspect jealousy with which, in the interest of her remnant of youth and beauty, she taxed her commerce with most of the fashionable sisterhood. She strove to repair her one notable grievance against fate by treating Nora as a daughter. She mused with real maternal ardour upon the young girl's matrimonial possibilities, and among them upon that design of which Roger had dropped her a hint of old. He held to his purpose of course; if he had fancied Nora then, he could but fancy her now.

But were his purpose and his fancy to be viewed with undiminished complacency? What might have been a great prospect for Nora as a plain homeless child, was a small prospect for a young lady who was turning out one of the beauties of the day. Roger would be the best of husbands; but in Mrs. Keith's philosophy a very good husband might represent a very indifferent marriage. She herself had married a fool, but she had married well. Her easy, opulent widowhood was there to show it. To call things by their names, would Nora, in marrying Roger, marry money? Mrs. Keith desired to appraise the worldly goods of her rejected suitor. At the time of his suit she had the matter at her fingers' ends; but she suspected that since then he had been lining his pockets. He puzzled her; he had a way of seeming neither rich nor poor. When he spent largely, he had the air of a man straining a point; yet when he abstained, it seemed rather from taste than from necessity. She had been surprised more than once, while abroad, by his copious remittances to Nora. The point was worth making sure of. The reader will agree with me that her conclusion warranted her friend either a fool or a hero; for she graciously assumed that if, financially, Roger should be found wanting, she could easily prevail upon him to make way for a millionaire. She had several millionaires in her eye. Never was better evidence that Roger passed for a good fellow. In any event, however, Mrs. Keith had no favour to spare for Hubert and his marked and increasing "attentions." She had determined to beware of false alarms; but meanwhile she was vigilant. Hubert presented himself daily with a report of his cousin's condition,—a report most minute and exhaustive, seemingly, as a couple of hours were needed to make it. Nora, moreover went frequently to her friend's house, wandered about aimlessly, and talked with Lucinda; and here Hubert coming on the same errand, was sure to be found or to find her. Roger's malady had defined itself as virulent typhus fever; strength and reason were at the lowest ebb. Of course on these occasions Hubert walked home with the young girl; and as the autumn weather made walking delightful, they chose the longest way. They might have been seen at this period perambulating in deep discourse certain outlying regions, the connection of which with the main line of travel between Mrs. Keith's abode and Roger's was not immediately obvious. Apart from her prudent fears, Mrs. Keith had a scantier kindness for Hubert than for most brilliant men. "What is he, when you come to the point?" she impatiently demanded of a friend to whom she had imparted her fears. "He is neither fish nor flesh, neither a priest nor a layman. I like a clergyman to bring with him a little odour of sanctity,—something that rests you, after all your bother. Nothing is so pleasant, near the fire, at the sober end of one's drawing-room. If he doesn't fill a certain place, he is in the way. The Reverend Hubert is in any place and every place. His manners are neither of this world nor, I hope, of the next. Last night he let me bring him a cup of tea and sat lounging in his chair while I put it into his hand. O, he knows what he's about. He is pretentious, with all his nonchalance. He finds the prayer-book rather meagre fare for week-days; so he consoles himself with his pretty parishioners. To be a parishioner, you needn't go to his church."

But in spite of Mrs. Keith's sceptical criticism, these young persons played their game in their own way, with wider moves, even, and heavier stakes, than their shrewd hostess suspected. As Nora, for the present, declined all invitations, Mrs. Keith in the evening frequently went out alone, leaving her in the drawing-room to entertain Hubert Lawrence. Roger's illness furnished a grave undercurrent to their talk and gave it a tone of hazardous melancholy. Nora's young life had known no such hours as these. She hardly knew, perhaps, just what made them what they were. She hardly wished to know; she shrank from breaking the charm with a question. The scenes of the past year had gathered into the background like a huge distant landscape, glowing with colour and swarming with life; she seemed to stand with her friend in the shadow of a passing cloud, looking off into the mighty picture, caressing its fine outlines and lingering where the haze of regret lay purple in its hollows. Hubert, meanwhile, told over the legends of town and tower, of hill and stream. Never, she fondly fancied, had a young couple conversed with less of narrow exclusiveness; they took all history, all culture, into their confidence; the radiant light of an immense horizon seemed to shine between them. Nora had felt perfectly satisfied; she seemed to live equally in every need of her being, in soul and sense, in heart and mind. As for Hubert, he knew nothing, for the time, save that the angel was within his gates and must be treated to angelic fare. He had for the time the conscience or the no-conscience, of a man who is feasting in Elysian meadows. He thought no evil; he designed no harm; the hard face of destiny was twisted into a smile. If only, for Hubert's sake, this had been an irresponsible world, without penalties to pay, without turnings to the longest lanes! If the peaches and plums in the garden of pleasure had no cheeks but ripe ones, and if, when we have eaten the fruit, we had not to dispose of the stones! Nora's charm of charms was a certain maidenly reserve which Hubert both longed and feared to abolish. While it soothed his conscience it irritated his ambition. He wished to know in what depth of water he stood; but there was no tell-tale ripple in this tropic calm. Was he drifting in mid-ocean, or was he cruising idly among the sandy shallows? As the days elapsed, he found his rest troubled by this folded rose-leaf of doubt; for he was not used to being baffled by feminine riddles. He determined to pluck out the heart of the mystery.

One evening, at Mrs. Keith's urgent request, Nora had prepared to go to the opera, as the season was to be very brief. Mrs. Keith was to dine with some friends and go thither in their company; one of the ladies was to call for Nora after dinner, and they were to join the party at the theatre. In the afternoon there came to Mrs. Keith's a young German lady, a pianist of merit who had her way to make, a niece of Nora's regular professor, with whom Nora had an engagement to practise duets twice a week. It so happened that, owing to a violent rain, Miss Lilienthal had been unable to depart after their playing; whereupon Nora had kept her to dinner, and the two, over their sweetbread, had sworn an eternal friendship. After dinner Nora went up to dress for the opera, and, on descending, found Hubert sitting by the fire deep in German discourse with the musical stranger. "I was afraid you would be going," said Hubert; "I saw *Der Freyschütz* on the placards. Well, lots of pleasure! Let me stay here awhile and polish up my German with Mademoiselle. It is great fun. And when the rain is over, Fräulein, perhaps you'll not mind my walking home with you."

But Mademoiselle was gazing in mute envy at Nora, standing before her in festal array. "She can take the carriage," said Nora, "when we have used it." And then reading the burden of that wistful regard—"Have you never heard *Der Freyschütz*?"

"Often!" said the other, with a poignant smile.

Nora reflected a moment, then drew off her gloves. "You shall go, you shall take my place. I will stay at home. Your dress will do; you shall wear my shawl. Let me put this flower into your hair, and here are my gloves and my fan. So! You are charming. My gloves are large,

—never mind. The others will be delighted to have you; come to-morrow and tell me all about it." Nora's friend, in her carriage, was already at the door. The gentle Fräulein, half shrinking, half eager, suffered herself to be hurried down to the carriage. On the doorstep she turned and kissed her hostess with a fervent "*Du allerliebste!*" Hubert wondered whether Nora's purpose had been to please her friend or to please herself. Was it that she preferred his society to Weber's music? He knew that she had a passion for Weber. "You have lost the opera," he said, when she reappeared; "but let us have an opera of our own. Play something; play Weber." So she played Weber for more than an hour; and I doubt whether, among the singers who filled the theatre with their melody, the master found that evening a truer interpreter than the young girl playing in the lamplit parlour to the man she loved. She played herself tired. "You ought to be extremely grateful," she said, as she struck the last chord; "I have never played so well."

Later they came to speak of a novel which lay on the table, and which Nora had been reading. "It is very silly," she said, "but I go on with it in spite of myself. I am afraid I am too easily pleased; no novel is so silly I can't read it. I recommend you this, by the way. The hero is a young clergyman, endowed with every charm, who falls in love with a Roman Catholic. She is rather a bigot, and though she loves the young man, she loves her religion better. To win his suit he comes near going over to Rome; but he pulls up short and determines the mountain shall come to Mahomet. He sets bravely to work, converts the young lady, baptizes her one week and marries her the next."

"Heaven preserve us, what a hotch-potch!" cried Hubert. "Is that what they are writing nowadays? I very seldom read a novel, but when I glance into one, I am sure to find some such stuff as that! Nothing irritates me so as the flatness of people's imagination. Common life,—I don't say it's a vision of bliss, but it's better than that. Their stories are like the underside of a carpet,— nothing but the stringy grain of the tissue,—a muddle of figures without shape and flowers without colour. When I read a novel my imagination starts off at a gallop and leaves the narrator hidden in a cloud of dust; I have to come jogging twenty miles back to the dénouement. Your clergyman here with his Romish sweetheart must be a very poor creature. Why didn't he marry her first and convert her afterwards? Isn't a clergyman after all, before all, a man? I mean to write a novel about a priest who falls in love with a pretty Mahometan and swears by Allah to win her."

"O Hubert!" cried Nora, "would you like a clergyman to love a pretty Mahometan better than the truth?"

"The truth? A pretty Mahometan may be the truth. If you can get it in the concrete, after shivering all your days in the cold abstract, it's worth a bit of a compromise. Nora, Nora!" he went on, stretching himself back on the sofa and flinging one arm over his head, "I stand up for passion! If a thing can take the shape of passion, that's a fact in its favour. The greater passion is the better cause. If my love wrestles with my faith, as the angel with

Jacob, and if my love stands uppermost, I will admit it's a fair game. Faith is faith, under a hundred forms! Upon my word, I should like to prove it. What a fraction of my personality is this clerical title! How little it expresses; how little it covers! On Sundays, in the pulpit, I stand up and talk to five hundred people. Does each of them, think you, appropriate his five hundredth share of my discourse? I can imagine talking to one person and saying five hundred times as much, even though she were a pretty Mahometan or a prepossessing idolatress! I can imagine being five thousand miles away from this blessed Boston,—in Turkish trousers, if you please, with a turban on my head and a chibouque in my mouth, with a great blue ball of Eastern sky staring in through the round window, high up; all in perfect indifference to the fact that Boston was abusing or, worse still, forgetting me! But my dear Nora," Hubert added, suddenly, "don't let me introduce confusion into your ideas." And he left his sofa and came and leaned against the mantel-shelf. "This is between ourselves; I talk to you as I would to no one else. Understand me and forgive me! There are times when I must speak out and pay my respects to the possible, the ideal! I must protest against the vulgar assumption of people who don't see beyond their noses; that people who do, you and I for instance, are living up to the top of our capacity; that we are contented, satisfied, balanced. I promise you I am not satisfied, not I! I have room for more. I only half live; I am like a purse filled at one end with small coin and empty at the other. Perhaps the other will never know the golden rattle! The

Lord's will be done; I can say that with the best of them. But I shall never pretend that I have known happiness, that I have known life. On the contrary, I shall maintain I am a failure. I had the wit to see, but I lacked the courage to do,—and yet I have been called reckless, irreverent, audacious. My dear Nora, I am the veriest coward on earth; pity me, if you don't despise me. There are men born to imagine things, others born to do them. Evidently I am not one of the doers. But I imagine things, I assure you!"

Nora listened to this flow of sweet unreason without staying her hand in the work, which, as she perceived the drift of his talk, she had rapidly caught up, but with a beating heart and a sense of rising tears. It was a ravishing mixture of passion and reason, the agony of a restless soul. Of old, she had thought of Hubert's nature as immutably placid and fixed; it gave her the notion of lucid depth and soundless volume. But of late, with greater nearness, she had seen the ripples on its surface and heard it beating its banks. This was not the first time; but the waves had never yet broken so high; she had never felt their salt spray on her cheeks. The touch of it now was delicious. She went on with her work, mechanically taking her stitches. She felt Hubert's intense blue eyes; the little blue flower in her tapestry grew under her quick needle. A door had suddenly been opened between their hearts; she passed through it. "What is it you imagine," she asked, with intense curiosity; "what is it you dream of doing?"

"I dream," he said, "of breaking some law for your sake!"

The answer frightened her; passion was outstripping reason. What had she to do with broken laws? She trembled and rolled up her work. "I dream," she said, trying to smile, "of the beauty of keeping laws. I expect to get a deal of pleasure from it yet." And she left her chair. For an instant Hubert was confused. Was this the last struggle which precedes submission, or the mere prudence of indifference? Nora's eyes were on the clock. It rang out eleven. "To begin with," she said, "let me keep the law of going early to bed. Good-night!"

Hubert wondered; he hardly knew whether this was a rebuke or a challenge. "You will at least shake hands," he said reproachfully.

She had meant in self-defence to omit this ceremony, but she let him take her hand. Hubert gazed at her a moment and raised it to his lips. She blushed, and rapidly withdrew it. "There!" cried Hubert, "I have broken a law!"

"Much good may it do you!" she answered, and went her way. He stood for a moment, waiting, and fancying, rather fatuously, that she might come back. Then, as he took up his hat, he wondered whether she too was not a bit of a coquette.

Nora wondered on her own side whether this scene had not been a little pre-arranged. For a day love and doubt fared in company. Lucinda's mournful discourse on the morrow was not of a nature to restore her calmness. "Last night," said Roger's nurse, "he was very bad. He woke up out of his stupor, but he was none the better for that. He talked all night about you. If he murmurs a word, it's always your name. He asked a dozen times if you had arrived, and forgot as often as I told him,—he, dear man, who used to remember the very hairs of your head. He kept wondering whether anything had happened to you. Late in the evening, when the carriages began to pass, he cried out that each of them was you, and what would you think of him for not coming to meet you? 'Don't tell her how bad I am,' he says; 'I must have been in bed two or three days, haven't I, Lucinda? Say I shall be out to-morrow; that I have only a little cold. Hubert will do everything for her,' he kept saying. And then when, at midnight, the wind began to blow, he declared it was a storm, that your ship was on the coast. God keep you safe, he cried. Then he asked if you were changed and grown; were you pretty, were you tall, should he know you? And he took the hand-glass and looked at himself and wondered if you would know him. He cried out that he was ugly, he was horrible, you would hate him. He bade me bring him his dressing things so that he might make himself look better, and when I wouldn't, he began to rage and call me names, and then he broke down and cried like a child." Hearing these things, Nora prayed intently for Roger's recovery, —prayed that he might live to see her more cunningly and lovingly his debtor. She wished to do something, she hardly knew what, not only to prove, but for ever to commemorate, her devotion. She felt capable of erecting a monument of self-sacrifice. Her conscience was perfectly at rest.

For a couple of days she saw nothing of Hubert. On

the third there came excellent news of Roger, who had taken a marked turn for the better, and had passed the crisis. She had declined, for the evening, a certain attractive invitation; but on the receipt of these tidings she revoked her refusal. Coming down to the drawing-room with Mrs. Keith, dressed and shawled, she found Hubert in waiting, with a face which uttered bad news. Roger's improvement had been momentary, a relapse had followed, and he was worse than ever. She tossed off her shawl with an energy not unnoted by her duenna. "Of course I cannot go," she said. "It is neither possible nor proper." Mrs. Keith would have given her biggest bracelet that this thing should not have happened in just this way; but she submitted with a good grace,—for a duenna. Hubert went down with her to her carriage. At the foot of the stairs she stopped, and while gathering up her skirts, "Mr. Lawrence," she demanded, "are you going to remain here?"

"A little while," said Hubert, with his imperturbable smile.

"A very little while, I hope." She had been wondering whether admonition would serve as a check or a stimulus. "I need hardly tell you that the young lady upstairs is not a person to be trifled with."

"I hardly know what you mean," said Hubert. "Am I a person to trifle?"

"Is it serious, then?"

Hubert hesitated a moment. She perceived a sudden watchful quiver in his eye, like a sword turned edge outward. She unsheathed one of her own steely beams, and for the tenth of a second there was a dainty crossing of blades. "I admire Miss Lambert," cried Hubert, "with all my heart."

"True admiration," said Mrs. Keith, "is one half respect and the other half self-denial."

Hubert laughed, ever so politely. "I will put that into a sermon," he said.

"O, I have a sermon to preach you," she answered. "Take your hat and go."

He looked very grave: "I will go up and get my hat." Mrs. Keith, catching his eye as he closed the carriage door, wished to Heaven that she had held her tongue. "I have done him injustice," she murmured as she went. "I have fancied him light, but I see he's vicious," Hubert, however, kept his promise in so far as that he did take up his hat. Having held it a moment he put it down. He had reckoned without his hostess! Nora was seated by the fire, with her bare arms folded, with a downcast brow. Dressed in pale corn-colour, her white throat confined by a band of blue velvet overstitched with a dozen pearls, she was not a subject for summary fare-wells. Meeting her eyes, he saw they were filled with tears. "You must not take this thing too hard," he said.

For a moment she answered nothing; then she bent her face into her hands and her tears flowed. "O poor, poor Roger!" she cried.

Hubert watched her weeping in her ball-dress those primitive tears. "I have not given him up," he said at last. "But suppose I had——" She raised her head and looked at him. "O," he cried, "I should have a hundred things to say! Both as a clergyman and as a man, I should preach resignation. In this crisis, let me speak my mind. Roger is part of your childhood; your childhood's at an end. Possibly, with it he too is to go! At all events you are not to feel that in losing him you lose everything. I protest! As you sit here he belongs to your past. Ask yourself what part he may play in your future. Believe me, you will have to settle it, you will have to choose. Here, in any case, *your* life begins. Your tears are for the dead past; this is the future, with its living needs. Roger's fate is only one of them."

She rose with her tears replaced by a passionate gravity. "Ah, you don't know what you say!" she cried. "Talk of my future if you like, but not of my past! No one can speak of it, no one knows it! Such as you see me here, bedecked and bedizened, I am a penniless, homeless, friendless creature! But for Roger, I might be in the streets! Do you think I have forgotten it, that I ever can forget it? There are things that colour one's life, memories that last for ever. I have my share! What am I to settle, between whom am I to choose? My love for Roger is no choice, it is part and parcel of my being!"

Hubert was inspired; he forgot everything but that she was lovely. "I wish to Heaven," he cried, "that you had never ceased to be penniless and friendless! I wish Roger had left you alone and not smothered you beneath this terrible burden of gratitude! Give him back his gifts! Take all *I* have! In the streets? In the streets I should have found you, as lovely in your poverty as you are now in your finery, and a thousand times more free!"

He seized her hand and met her eyes with irresistible ardour. Pain and pleasure, at once, possessed Nora's heart. It was as if joy, bursting in, had trampled certain tender flowers that bloomed on the threshold. But Hubert had cried, "I love you! I love you!" and joy had taken up the words. She was unable to speak audibly; but in an instant she was spared the effort. The servant hastily came in with a note superscribed with her name. She motioned to Hubert to open it. He read it aloud. "Mr. Lawrence is sinking. You had better come. I send my carriage." Nora's voice came to her with a cry,— "He is dying, he is dying!"

In a minute's time she found herself wrapped in her shawl and seated with Hubert in the doctor's coupé. A few moments more and the doctor received them at the door of Roger's room. They passed in, and Nora went straight to the bed. Hubert stood an instant and saw her drop on her knees beside the pillow. She flung back her shawl with vehemence, as if to release her arms; she was throwing them round her friend. Hubert went on into the adjoining chamber, of which the door stood open. The room was dark, the other lit by a night-lamp. He stood listening awhile, but heard nothing; then he began to walk slowly to and fro, past the doorway. He could see nothing but the shining train of Nora's dress lying on the carpet beyond the angle of the bed. He wanted terribly to see more, but he feared to see too much. At moments he thought he heard whispers. This lasted some time; then the doctor came in, with what seemed to him an odd, unprofessional smile. "The young lady knows a few remedies not taught in the schools," he whispered "He has recognised her. He is good for to-night, at least. Half an hour ago he had no pulse at all, but this has started it. I will come back in an hour." After he had gone Lucinda came, self-commissioned, and shut the door in Hubert's face. He stood a moment, with an unreasoned sense of insult and defeat. Then he walked straight out of the house. But the next morning, after breakfast, a more generous sentiment moved him to return. The doctor was just coming away. "It was a Daniel come to judgement," the doctor declared. "I verily believe she saved him. He will be sitting up in a fortnight." Hubert learned that, having achieved her miracle, Nora had returned to Mrs. Keith's. What arts she had used he was left to imagine. He had still a sore feeling of having just missed a crowning joy; but there might yet be time to grasp it. He felt, too, an urgent need of catching a glimpse of the afterglow of Nora's mystical effluence. He repaired to Mrs. Keith's hoping to find the young girl alone. But the elder lady, as luck would have it, was established in the drawing-room, and she made haste to inform him that Nora, fatigued by her "watching," had not yet left her room. But if Hubert was sombre, Mrs. Keith was radiant. Now was her chance to preach her promised sermon; she had just come into possession of facts that furnished a capital text.

"I suppose you will call me a meddling busybody," she said. "I confess I seem to myself a model of for-bearance. Be so good as to tell me in three words whether you are in love with Nora."

Taken thus abruptly to task, Hubert, after a moment's trepidation, kept his balance. He measured the situation at a glance, and pronounced it bad. But if heroic urbanity would save it, he would be urbane. "It is hardly a question to answer in two words," he answered, with an ingenuous smile. "I wish you could tell me!"

"Really," said Mrs. Keith, "it seems to me that by this time you might know. Tell me at least whether you are prepared to marry her?"

Hubert hesitated just an instant. "Of course not,—so long as I am not sure I am in love with her!"

"And pray when will you make up your mind? And what is to become of poor Nora meanwhile?"

"Why, Mrs. Keith, if Nora can wait, surely you can." The urbanity need not be all on his side.

"Nora can wait? That's easily said. Is a young girl a thing to be tried like a piano,—to be strummed on for a pretty tune? O Mr. Lawrence, if I had ever doubted of the selfishness of men! What this matter has been for you, you know best yourself; but I may tell you that for Nora it has been serious." At these words Hubert passed his hand nervously through his hair and walked to the window. "The miserable fop!" said Mrs. Keith privately. "His vanity is the only thing that has ears. It is very true they are long ones! If you are not able to make Nora a handsome offer of marriage," she proceeded, "you have no business here. Retire, quietly, expeditiously, humbly. Leave Nora to me. I will heal her bruises. They shall have been wholesome ones."

Hubert felt that these peremptory accents implied a

menace, and that the lady spoke by book. His vanity rankled, but discretion drew a long breath. For a fortnight it had been shut up in a closet. He thanked his stars they had no witnesses; from Mrs. Keith, for once, he could afford to take a lesson. He remained silent for a moment, with his brow bent in meditation. Then turning suddenly, he faced the music. "Mrs. Keith," he said, "you have done me a service. I thank you sincerely. I have gone further than I meant; I admit it. I am selfish, I am vain, I am anything you please. My only excuse is Nora's loveliness. It had made an ass of me; I had forgotten that this is a life of logic." And he bravely took up his hat.

Mrs. Keith was prepared for a "scene"; she was annoyed at missing it, and her easy triumph led her on. She thought, too, of the young girl upstairs, combing out her golden hair, and seeing no logic in her looking-glass. She had dragged a heavy gun to the front; she determined to fire her shot. So much virtue had never inspired her with so little respect. She played a moment with the bow on her morning-dress. "Let me thank you for your great humility," she said. "Do you know I was going to be afraid of you, so that I had entrenched myself behind a great big preposterous fact? I met, last evening, Mrs. Chatterton of New York. You know she's a great talker, but she talks to the point. She mentioned your engagement to a certain young lady, a dark-eyed person, —need I repeat the name?" There was no need of her repeating names; Hubert stood before her, flushing crimson, with his blue eyes flashing cold wrath. He remained

174

silent a moment, shaking a scornful finger at her. "For shame, madam," he cried. "That's in shocking taste! You might have been generous; it seems to me I deserve it." And with a summary bow he departed.

Mrs. Keith repented of this extra touch of zeal; the more so as she found that, practically, Nora was to be the victim of the young man's displeasure. For four days he gave no sign; Nora was left to explain his absence as she might. Even Roger's amendment failed to console her. At last, as the two ladies were sitting at lunch, his card was brought in, superscribed *P.P.C.* Nora read it in silence, and for a moment rested her eyes on her companion with a piteous look which seemed to ask, "Is it *you* I have to thank for this?" A torrent of remonstrances rose to Nora's lips, but they were sealed by the reflection that, though her friend might have been concerned in Hubert's desertion, its peculiar abruptness had a peculiar motive. She pretended to occupy herself with her plate; but her self-control was rapidly ebbing. She silently rose and retreated to her own room, leaving Mrs. Keith moralising, over her mutton-chop, upon the miseries of young-ladyhood and the immeasurable egotism of the man who would rather produce a cruel effect than none at all. For a week after this Nora was seriously ill. On the day she left her room she received a short note from Hubert.

NEW YORK.

DEAR NORA—You have, I suppose, been expecting to hear from me; but I have not written, because I am unable to write as I wish and unwilling to write as—other people would wish!

I left Boston suddenly, but not unadvisedly. I shall for the present be occupied here. The last month I spent there will remain one of the best memories of my life. But it was time it should end! Remember me a little—what do I say?—forget me! Farewell. I received this morning from the doctor the best accounts of Roger.

Nora handled this letter somewhat as one may imagine a pious maiden of the antique world to have treated a messenger from the Delphic oracle. It was obscure, it was even sinister; but deep in its sacred dimness there seemed to glow a fiery particle of truth. She locked it up in her dressing-case and wondered and waited. Shortly after came a missive of a different cast. It was from her cousin, George Fenton, and also dated New York.

DEAR NORA—You have left me to find out your return in the papers. I saw your name a month ago in the steamer's list. But I hope the fine people and things you have been seeing haven't drive me quite out of your heart,—that you remember at least who I am. I received your answer to my letter of last February; after which I immediately wrote again, but in vain! Perhaps you never got my letter; I could scarcely decipher your Italian address. Excuse my want of learning! Your photograph is a joy for ever. Are you really as handsome as that? It taxes even the credulity of one who knows how pretty you used to be; how good you must be still. When I last wrote I told you of my having taken stock in an enterprise for working over refuse iron. But what do you care for refuse iron! It's awfully dirty, and not fit to be talked of to a fine lady like you. Still, if you have any odd bits,—old keys, old nails,— the smallest contributions thankfully received! We think there is money in it; if there isn't, I'm afloat again. If this fails, I think of going to Texas. I wish I might see you first. Get Mr. Lawrence to bring you to New York for a week. I suppose it wouldn't do for me to call on you in the light of day; but I might hang round your hotel and see you going in and out. Does he love me as much as ever, Mr. Lawrence? Poor man, tell him to take it easy; I shall never trouble him again. Are you ever lonely in the midst of your grandeur? Do you ever feel that, after all, these people are not of your blood and bone? I should like you to quarrel with them, to know a day's friendlessness or a day's freedom, so that you might remember that here in New York, in a dusty iron-yard, there is a poor devil who is your natural protector.

VIII

ROGER'S convalescence went smoothly forward. One morning as he lay coquetting deliciously with returning sense, he became aware that a woman was sitting at his window in the sun. She seemed to be reading. He fancied vaguely that she was Lucinda; but at last it occurred to him that Lucinda was not addicted to literature, and that Lucinda's tresses, catching the light were not of a kind to take on the likeness of a queenly crown. She was no vision; his visions had been dark and troubled; and this image was radiant and fixed. He half closed his eyes and watched her lazily through the lids. There came to him, out of his boyish past, a vague, delightful echo of the "Arabian Nights." The room was gilded by the autumn sunshine into the semblance of an enamelled harem court; he himself seemed a languid Persian, lounging on musky cushions; the fair woman at the window a Scheherazade, a Badoura. He closed his eyes completely and gave a little groan, to see if she would move. When he opened them, she had moved; she stood near his bed, looking at him. For a moment his puzzled gaze still told him nothing but that she was fictitiously fair. She smiled and smiled, and, after a little, as he only stared confusedly, she blushed, not like Badoura or Scheherazade, but like Nora. Her frequent presence after this became the great fact in his convalescence. The thought of her beauty filled the long empty hours during which he was forbidden to do anything but grow strong. Sometimes he wondered whether his impression of it was only part of the universal optimism of a man with a raging appetite. Then he would question Lucinda, who would shake her head and chuckle with elderly archness. "Wait till you are on your feet, sir, and judge for yourself," she would say. "Go and call on her at Mrs. Keith's, and then tell me what you think." He grew well with a beating heart; he would have stayed his recovery for the very dread of facing his happiness. But at last, one Sunday, he discarded his dressing-gown and sat up, clothed and in his right mind. The effort, of course, gave him a huge appetite, and he dealt vigorous justice upon his luncheon. He had just finished, and his little table was still in position near his arm-chair, when Nora made her appearance. She had been to church, and on leaving church had taken a long walk. She wore one of those dark rich toilets of early winter that are so becoming to fair beauties; but her face lacked freshness; she was pale and tired. On Roger's remarking it, she said the service had given her a headache; as a remedy, she had marched off briskly at haphazard, missed her way, and wandered hither and thither. But here she was, safe and sound and hungry. She asked for a share of Roger's luncheon, and, taking off her bonnet, was bountifully served at his table. She ate largely and hungrily, jesting at her appetite and getting back her colour. Roger leaned back in his chair, watching her, carving her partridge, offering her this and that; in a word, falling in love. It happened as naturally as if he had never allowed for it. The flower of her beauty had bloomed in a night, that of his passion in a day. When at last she laid down her fork, and, sinking back in her chair, folded her hands on her arms and sat facing him with a friendly, pointless, satisfied smile, and then, raising her goblet, threw back her head and showed her white throat and glanced at him over the brim, while he noted her plump ringless hand, with the little finger curled out, he felt that he was in health again. She strolled about the room, idly touching the instruments on his dressing-table and the odds and ends on his chimney-piece. Her dress, which she had released from the loops and festoons then in fashion, trailed rustling on the carpet, and lent her a sumptuous, ladyish air which seemed to give a price to this domiciliary visit. "Everywhere, everywhere, a little dust," she said. "I see it is more than time I should be back here. I have been waiting for you to invite me; but as you don't seem inclined, I invite myself."

Roger said nothing for a moment. Then with a blush, "I don't mean to invite you; I don't want you."

Nora stared. "Don't want me? *Par exemple!*"

"I want you as a visitor; but not as a——" And he fumbled for his word.

"As a resident?" She took it gaily. "You turn me out of doors?"

"No; I don't take you in—yet awhile. My dear child, I have a reason."

Nora wondered, still smiling. "I might consider this very unkind," she said, "if I had not the patience of an angel. Would you kindly mention your reason?"

"Not now," he answered. "But never fear, when it

comes it will be all-sufficient!" But he imparted it, a couple of days after, to Mrs. Keith, who came late in the afternoon to present her compliments on his recovery. She displayed an almost sisterly graciousness, enhanced by a lingering spice of coquetry; but somehow, as she talked, he felt as if she were an old woman and he still a young man. It seemed a sort of hearsay that they should ever have been mistress and lover. "Nora will have told you," he said, "of my wishing you kindly to keep her awhile longer. I can give you no better proof of my regard, for the fact is, my dear friend, I am in love with her."

"Come!" she cried. "This is interesting."

"I wish her to accept me freely, as she would accept any other man. For that purpose I must cease to be, in all personal matters, her guardian."

"She must herself forget her wardship, if there is to be any sentimentalising between you,—all but forget it, at least. Let me speak frankly," she went on. Whereupon Roger frowned a bit, for he had known her frankness to be somewhat incisive. "It is all very well that you should be in love with her. You are not the first. Don't be frightened; your chance is fair. The needful point is that she should be just the least bit in love with you."

He shook his head with melancholy modesty. "I don't expect that. She loves me a little, I hope; but I say nothing to her imagination. Circumstances are fatally against it. If she falls in love, it will be with a man as unlike me as possible. Nevertheless, I do hope she may, without pain, learn to think of me as a husband. I hope," he cried, with appealing eyes, "that she may see a certain rough propriety in it. After all, who can make her such a husband as I? I am neither handsome, nor clever, nor accomplished, nor celebrated. She might choose from a dozen men who are. Pretty lovers doubtless they would make; but, my friend, it's the *husband*, the husband, that is the test!" And he beat his clenched hand on his knee. "Do they know her, have they watched her, as I have done? What are their months to my years, their vows to my acts? Mrs. Keith!"—and he grasped her hand as if to call her to witness,—"I undertake to make her happy. I know what you can say,—that a woman's happiness is worth nothing unless imagination lends a hand. Well, even as a lover, perhaps I am not a hopeless case! And then, I confess, other things being equal, I would rather Nora should not marry a poor man."

Mrs. Keith spoke, on this hint. "You are a rich one, then?"

Roger folded up his pocket-handkerchief and patted it out on his knee, with pregnant hesitation. "Yes, I am rich,—I may call it so. I am rich!" he repeated with unction. "I can say it at last." He paused a moment, and then, with unstudied irony,—"I was not altogether a pauper when you refused me. Since then, for the last six years, I have been saving and sparing and counting. My purpose has sharpened my wits, and fortune, too, has favoured me. I have speculated a little, I have handled stock and turned this and that about, and now I can offer my wife a very pretty fortune. It has been going on very quietly; people don't know it; but Nora, if she cares to, shall show them!" Mrs. Keith coloured and mused; she was lost in a tardy afterthought. "It seems odd to be talking to you this way," Roger went on, exhilarated by this summing-up of his career. "Do you remember that letter of mine from P——?"

"I did not tear it up in a rage," she answered. "I came across it the other day."

"It was rather odd, my writing it, you know," Roger confessed. "But in my sudden desire to register a vow, I needed a friend. I turned to you as my best friend." Mrs. Keith acknowledged the honour with a toss of her head. Had she made a mistake of old? She very soon decided that Nora should not repeat it. Her hand-shake, as she left her friend, was generous; it seemed to assure him that he might count upon her.

When, soon after, he made his appearance in her drawing-room, she gave him many a hint as to how to play his cards. But he irritated her by his slowness; he was too circumspect by half. It was only in the evening that he took a hand in the game. During the day he left Nora to her own affairs, and was in general neither more nor less attentive than if he had been a merely susceptible stranger. To spectators his present relation with the young girl was somewhat puzzling; though Mrs. Keith, by no ambiguous giving out, as Hamlet says, had diffused a sympathetic expectancy. Roger wondered again and again whether Nora had guessed his meaning. He observed in her at times, as he fancied, a sort of nervous levity which seemed born of a need to conjure away the phantom of sentiment. And of this hostile need, of course, he hereupon strove to trace the lineage. He talked with her little, as yet, and never interfered in her talk with others; but he watched her devotedly from corners, and caught her words through the hum of voices. Sometimes she looked at him as if she were on the point of telling him something. What had she to tell him? In trying to guess, Roger made up his mind that she was in love. Search as he could, however, he was unable to find her lover. It was no one there present; they were all alike wasting their shot; the enemy had stolen a march and was hidden in the very heart of the citadel. He appealed distractedly to Mrs. Keith. "Lovesick,—lovesick is the word," he groaned. "I have read of it all my days in the poets, but here it is in the flesh. The poor girl plays her part well; she's wound up tight; but the spring will snap and the watch run down. D——n the man! I would rather he carried her off than sit and see this." He saw that his friend had bad news. "Tell me everything," he said; "don't spare me."

"You have noticed it at last," she answered. "I was afraid you would. Well! he's not far to seek. Think it over; can't you guess? My dear Mr. Lawrence, you are celestially simple. Your cousin Hubert is not."

"Hubert!" Roger echoed, staring. A spasm passed over his face; his eyes flashed. At last he hung his head. "Dear, dear," he said; "have I done it all for Hubert?"

"Not if I can help it!" cried Mrs. Keith sharply. "She may not marry you; but, at the worst, she shall not marry him!"

Roger laid his hand on her arm; first heavily, then gently. "Dear friend, she must be happy, at any cost. If she loves Hubert, she must marry him. I will settle an income!"

Mrs. Keith gave his knuckles a great rap with her fan. "You will settle a fiddlestick! You will keep your money and you will marry Miss Nora. Leave it to me! If you have no regard for your rights, at least I have."

"Rights? what rights have I? I might have let her alone. I needn't have settled down on her in this deadly fashion. But Hubert's a happy man! Does he know it? You must write to him. I can't!"

Mrs. Keith burst into a ringing laugh. "Know it? You are amazing! Hadn't I better telegraph?"

Roger stared and frowned. "Does he suspect it, then?"

Mrs. Keith rolled up her eyes. "Come," she said, "we must begin at the beginning. When you speak of your cousin, you open up a gulf. There is not much in it, it's true; but it's a gulf. Your cousin is a humbug,—neither more nor less. Allow me; I know what I say. He knew, of course, of your plans for Nora?" Roger nodded. "Of course he did! He took his chance, therefore, while you were well out of the way. He lost no time, and if Nora is in love with him, he can tell you why. He knew that he could not marry her, that he should not, that he would not. But he made love to her, to pass the time. Happily, it passed soon. I had of course to be cautious; but as soon as I saw how things were going, I spoke, and spoke to the point. Though he's a humbug, he is not a fool; that that was all he needed. He made his excuses, such as they were! I shall know in future what to think of him."

Roger shook his head mournfully. "I am afraid it's not to be so easily settled. As you say, Hubert's a gulf. I never sounded it. The fact remains that they love each other. It's hard, but it's fatal."

Mrs. Keith lost patience. "Don't try the heroic; you will break down," she cried. "You are the best of men, but after all you are human. To begin with, Hubert doesn't love her. He loves no one but himself. Nora must find her happiness where women as good have found it before this, in a sound, sensible marriage. She cannot marry Hubert; he is engaged to another person. Yes, I have the facts; a young girl in New York with whom he has been off and on for a couple of years, but who holds him to his bargain. I wish her joy of it! He is not to be pitied; she is not Nora, but she is extremely fond of him, and she is to have money. So good-bye to Hubert. As for you, cut the knot! She's a bit sentimental just now; but one sentiment, at that age, is as good as another. And, my dear man, the girl has a conscience, it's to be hoped; give her a chance to show it. A word to the wise!"

Thus exhorted, Roger determined to act. The next day was a Sunday. While the ladies were at church he took up his position in their drawing-room. Nora came in alone; Mrs. Keith had made a pretext for ascending to her own room, where she waited with some solemnity. "I am glad to find you," Nora said. "I have been wanting particularly to speak to you. Is my probation not over? May not I now come back?"

"It's about that," he answered, "that I came to talk to you. The probation has been mine. Has it lasted long enough? Do you love me yet? Come back to me,—come back to me as my wife."

She looked at him, as he spoke, with a clear, unfrightened gaze, and, with his last words, broke frankly into a laugh. But as his own face was intensely grave, a gradual blush arrested her laugh. "Your wife, Roger?" she asked gently.

"My wife. I offer you my hand. Dear Nora, is it so incredible?"

To his uttermost meaning, somehow, her ear was still closed; she still took it as a jest. "Is that the only condition on which we can live together?" she asked.

"The only one,—for me!"

She looked at him, still sounding his eyes with her own. But his passion, merciful still, retreated before her frank doubt. "Ah," she said, smiling, "what a pity I have grown up!"

"Well," he said, "since you are grown we must make the best of it. Think of it, Nora, think of it. I am not so old, you know. I was young when we began. You know me so well; you would be safe. It would simplify matters vastly; it's at least worth thinking of," he went on, pleading for very tenderness, in this pitiful minor key. "I know it must seem odd; but I make you the offer!"

Nora was almost shocked. In this strange new character of a lover she seemed to see him eclipsed as a friend, now when, in the trouble of her love, she turned longingly to friendship. She was silent awhile, with her embarrassment. "Dear Roger," she answered, at last, "let me love you in the old, old way. Why need we change? Nothing is so good, so safe as that. I thank you from my heart for your offer. You have given me too much already. Marry any woman you please, and I will be her serving-maid."

He had no heart to meet her eyes; he had wrought his own fate. Mechanically, he took up his hat and turned away, without speaking. She looked at him an instant, uncertain, and then, loath to part with him so abruptly, she laid her arm round his neck. "You don't think me unkind?" she said. "I will do anything for you on earth"—*but that* was unspoken, yet Roger heard it. The dream of years was shattered; he felt sick; he was dumb. "You forgive me?" she went on. "O Roger, Roger!" and, with a strange inconsequence of lovingness, she dropped her head on his shoulder. He held her for a moment as close as he had held his hope, and then released her as suddenly as he had parted with it. Before she knew it, he was gone.

Nora drew a long breath. It had all come and gone so fast that she was bewildered. It had been what she had heard called a "chance." Suppose she had grasped at it? She felt a kind of relief in the thought that she had been wise. That she had been cruel, she never suspected. She watched Roger, from the window, cross the street and take his way up the sunny slope. Two ladies passed him, friends, as Nora saw; but he made no bow. Suddenly Nora's reflexions deepened and the scene became portentous. If she had been wrong, she had been horribly wrong. She hardly dared to think of it. She ascended to her own room, to take counsel of familiar privacy. In the hall, as she passed, she found Mrs. Keith at her open door. This lady put her arm round her waist, led her into the chamber toward the light. "Something has happened," she said, looking at her curiously.

"Yes, I have had an offer of marriage. From Roger."

"Well, well?" Mrs. Keith was puzzled by her face.

"Isn't it kind of him? To think he should have thought it necessary! It was soon settled."

"Settled, dearest? How?"

"Why—why——" And Nora began to smile the more resolutely, as her imagination had taken alarm. "I declined."

Mrs. Keith released her with a gesture almost tragical. "Declined? Unhappy girl!" The words were charged with a righteous indignation so unusual to the speaker that Nora's conscience took the hint.

She turned very pale. "What have I done?" she asked appealingly.

"Done, my dear? You have done a blind, cruel act! Look here." And Mrs. Keith having hastily ransacked a drawer, turned about with an open letter.

"Read that and repent."

Nora took the letter; it was old and crumpled, the ink faded. She glanced at the date,—that of her first school year. In a moment she had read to the closing sentence. "It will be my own fault if I have not a perfect wife." In a moment more its heavy meaning overwhelmed her; its vital spark flashed back over the interval of years. She seemed to see Roger's bent, stunned head in the street. Mrs. Keith was frightened at her work. Nora dropped the letter and stood staring, open-mouthed, pale as death, with her poor young face blank with horror.

IX

Nora frequently wondered in after years how that Sunday afternoon had worked itself away; how, through the tumult of amazement and grief, decision, illumination, action, had finally come. She had disembarrassed herself of a vague attempt of Mrs. Keith's towards some compensatory caress, and making her way half blindly to her own room, had sat down face to face with her trouble. Here, if ever, was thunder from a clear sky. Her friend's disclosure took time to swell to its full magnitude; for an hour she sat, half stunned, seeming to see it climb heaven-high and glare upon her like some monstrous blighting sun. Then at last she broke into a cry and wept. Her immense pain gushed and filtered through her heart, and passed out in shuddering sobs. The whole face of things was hideously altered; a sudden horror had sprung up in her innocent past, and it seemed to fling forward a shadow which made the future a blank darkness. She felt cruelly deluded and injured; the sense of suffered wrong absorbed for the time the thought of wrong inflicted. She was too weak for indignation, but she overflowed with delicate resentment. That Roger, whom all these years she had fancied as simple as charity, should have been as double as interest, should have played a part and laid a train, that she had been living in darkness, on illusion and lies, all this was an intolerable thing. And the worst was that she had been cheated of the chance to be really loyal. Why had he never told her that she wore a chain! Why, when he took her, had he not drawn up his terms and made his bargain? She would have kept the bargain to the letter; she would have taught herself to be his wife. Duty then would have been duty; sentiment would have been sentiment; her youth would not have been so wretchedly misspent. She would have given up her heart betimes; doubtless it would have learned to beat to a decent and satisfied measure; but now it had throbbed to a finer music, a melody that would ring in her ears for ever. Thinking of what her conscience might have done, however, brought her to thinking of what it might still do. While she turned in her pain, angrily questioning it, Mrs. Keith knocked at the door. Nora repaired to the dressing-glass, to efface the traces of her tears; and while she stood there, she saw in her open dressing-case her last letter from her cousin. It gave her the help she was vaguely groping for. By the time she had crossed the room and opened the door she had welcomed and blessed this help; and while she gravely shook her head in response to Mrs. Keith's softly urgent, "Nora, dear, won't you let me come to you?" she had passionately made it her own. "I would rather be alone," she said; "I thank you very much."

It was past six o'clock; Mrs. Keith was dressed for the evening. It was her gracious practice on Sundays to dine with her mother-in-law. Nora knew, therefore, that if her companion accepted this present dismissal, she would be alone for several hours.

"Can't I do something for you?" Mrs. Keith inquired soothingly.

"Nothing at all, thank you. You are very kind."

Mrs. Keith looked at her, wondering whether this was the irony of bitter grief; but a certain cold calmness in the young girl's face, overlying her agitation, seemed to intimate that she had taken a wise resolve. And, in fact, Nora was now soaring sublime on the wings of purpose, and viewed Mrs. Keith's offence as a diminished fact. Mrs. Keith took her hands. "Write him a line, my dear," she gently urged.

Nora nodded. "Yes, I will write him a line."

"And when I come back, it will be all over?"

"Yes,—all over."

"God bless you, my dear." And on this theological amenity the two women kissed and separated. Nora returned to her dressing-case and read over her cousin's letter. Its clear friendliness seemed to ring out audibly amid this appalling hush of familiar harmony. "I wish you might know a day's friendlessness or a day's freedom, —a poor devil who is your natural protector." Here was indeed the voice of nature, of predestined tenderness; if her cousin had been there Nora would have flung herself into his arms. She sat down at her writing-table, with her brow in her hands, light-headed with her passionate purpose, steadying herself to think. A day's freedom had come at last; a lifetime's freedom confronted her. For, as you will have guessed, immediate retrocession and departure had imperiously prescribed themselves. Until this had taken place, there could be nothing but deeper trouble.

On the old terms there could be no clearing up; she could speak to Roger again only in perfect independence. She must throw off those suffocating bounties which had been meant to bribe her to the service in which she had so miserably failed. Her failure now she felt no impulse to question, her decision no energy to revise. I shall have told my story ill if these things seem to lack logic. The fault lay deeper and dated from longer ago than her morning's words of denial. Roger and she shared it between them; it was a heavy burden for both.

She wrote her "line," as she had promised Mrs. Keith, rapidly, without erasure; then wrote another to Mrs. Keith, folded and directed them and laid them on her dressing-table. She remembered now, distinctly, that she had heard of a Sunday-evening train to New York. She hastened downstairs, found in a newspaper the railway advertisement, and learned that the train started at eight; satisfied herself, too, that the coast was clear of servants, and that she might depart unquestioned. She bade a gleeful farewell to her borrowed possessions,—unearned wages, ineffective lures. She exchanged the dress she had worn to church for an old black silk one, put a few articles of the first necessity into a small travelling-bag, and emptied her purse of all save a few dollars. Then bonneted, shawled, veiled, with her bag in her hand, she went forth into the street. She would begin as she would have to proceed; she started for the station, savingly, on foot. Happily it was not far off; she reached it through the wintry darkness, out of breath, but in safety. She seemed to feel about her, as she went, the old Bohemianism of her childhood; she was once more her father's daughter. She bought her ticket and found a seat in the train without adventure; with a sort of shame, in fact, that this great deed of hers should be so easy to do. But as the train rattled hideously through the long wakeful hours of the night, difficulties came thickly; in the mere oppression of her conscious purpose, in the keener vision at moments of Roger's distress, in a vague dread of the great unknown into which she was rushing. But she could do no other,—no other; with this refrain she lulled her doubts. It was strange how, as the night elapsed and her heart-beats seemed to keep time to the crashing swing of the train, her pity for Roger increased. It would have been an immense relief to be able to hate him. Her undiminished affection, forced back upon her heart, swelled and rankled there tormentingly. But if she was unable to hate Roger, she could at least abuse herself. Every circumstance of the last six years, in this new light, seemed to have taken on a vivid meaning,—a meaning that made a sort of crime of her own want of foreknowledge. She kept thinking of expiation and determined she would write to Miss Murray, her former school-mistress, and beg that she might come and teach little girls their scales. She kept her cousin's letter clinched in her hand; but even when she was not thinking of Roger she was not always thinking of Fenton. She could tell Hubert Lawrence now that she was as poor and friend-less as he had ever wished he could see her.

Toward morning she fell asleep for weariness. She was roused by a great tumult and the stopping of the train, which had arrived. She found with dismay that, as it was but seven o'clock, she had two or three hours on her hands. George would hardly be at his place of business before ten, and the interval seemed formidable. The dusk of a winter's morning lingered still, and increased her trouble. But she followed her companions and stood in the street. Half-a-dozen hackmen attacked her; a facetious gentleman, lighting a cigar, asked her if she wouldn't take a carriage with him.

She made her escape from the bustle and hurried along the street, praying to be unnoticed. She told herself sternly that now her difficulties had begun and must be bravely faced; but as she stood at the street-corner, beneath an unextinguished lamp, listening to the nascent hum of the town, she felt a most unreasoned sinking of the heart. A Dutch grocer, behind her, was beginning to open his shop; an ash-barrel stood beside her, and while she lingered an old woman with a filthy bag on her back came and poked in it with a stick; a policeman, muffled in a comforter, came lounging squarely along the pavement and took her slender measure with his hard official eye. What a hideous, sordid world! She was afraid to do anything but walk and walk. Fortunately, in New York, in the upper region, it is impossible to lose one's way; and she knew that by keeping downward and to the right she should reach her appointed refuge. The streets looked shabby and of ill-repute; the houses seemed mean and sinister. When, to fill her time, she stopped before the window of some small shop, the objects within seemed in their ugliness, to mock at her unnatural refinement. She must give that up. At last she began to feel faint and hungry, for she had fasted since the previous morning. She ventured into an establishment which had *Ladies' Café* inscribed in gilt letters on a blue tablet in the window, and justified its title by an exhibition of stale pies and fly-blown festoons of tissue-paper. On her request, humbly preferred, for a cup of tea, she was served staringly and condescendingly by a half-dressed young woman, with frowzy hair and tumid eyes. The tea was bad, yet Nora swallowed it, not to complicate the situation. The young woman had come and sat down at her table, handled her travelling-bag, and asked a number of plain questions; among others, if she wouldn't like to go up and lie down. "I guess it's a dollar," said this person, to conclude her achievements, alluding to the cup of tea. Nora came afterwards to a square, in which was an enclosure containing trees, a frozen fountain, thawing fast, and benches. She went in and sat down on one of the benches. Several of the others were occupied by shabby men, sullen with fasting, with their hands thrust deep into their pockets, swinging their feet for warmth. She felt a faint fellowship in their grim idleness; but the fact that they were all men and she the only woman, seemed to open out deeper depths in her loneliness. At last, when it was nine o'clock, she made her way to Tenth Avenue and to George's address. It was a neighbourhood of store-houses and lumber-yards, of wholesale traffic in articles she had never heard of, and of multitudinous carts, drawn up along the pavement. She found a large cheap-looking sign in black and white,—*Franks and Fenton.*

Beneath it was an alley, and at the end of this alley a small office which seemed to communicate with an extension of the precinct in the rear. The office was open; a small ragged boy was sweeping it with a broom. From him she learned that neither Franks nor Fenton had arrived, but that if she wanted, she might come in and wait. She sat down in a corner, tremulous with conjecture, and scanned the room, trying to bridge over this dull interval with some palpable memento of her cousin. But the desk, the stove, the iron safe, the chairs, the sordid ink-spotted walls, were as blank and impersonal as so many columns of figures. When at last the door opened and a man appeared, it was not Fenton, but, presumably, Franks. Mr. Franks was a small meagre man, with a whitish colouring, weak blue eyes and thin yellow whiskers, suffering apparently from some nervous malady. He nodded, he stumbled, he jerked his arms and legs about with pitiful comicality. He had a huge protuberant forehead, such a forehead as would have done honour to a Goethe or a Newton; but poor Mr. Franks must have been at best a man of latent genius. Superficially he was a very witless person. He informed Nora, on learning her errand, that his partner ("pardner," he called it) was gone to Williamsburg on business, and would not return till noon; meanwhile, was it anything *he* could do? Nora's heart sank at this vision of comfort still deferred; but she thanked Mr. Franks, and begged leave to sit in her corner and wait. Her presence seemed to redouble his agitation; she remained for an hour gazing in painful fascination at his unnatural shrugs and spasms, as he busied himself at his desk. The Muse of accounts, for poor Mr. Franks, was, in fact, not habitually a young woman, thrice beautiful with trouble, sitting so sensibly at his elbow. Nora wondered how George had come to choose so foolish an associate; then she guessed that it was his want of capital that had discovered a secret affinity with Mr. Franks's want of brains. The merciless intensity of thought begotten by her excitement suggested that there was something dishonourable in this connection. From time to time Mr. Franks wheeled about in his chair and fixed her solemnly with his pallid glance, as if to offer her the privilege of telling him her story; and on her failure to avail herself of it, turned back to his ledger with a little grunt of injury and a renewal of his grotesque agitation. As the morning wore away, various gentlemen of the kind designated as "parties" came in and demanded Fenton in a tone that made the smallest possible account of Mr. Franks. Several of them sat awhile on tilted chairs, chewing their toothpicks, stroking their beards, and listening with a half-bored grin to what appeared to be an intensely confidential exposition of Mr. Franks's wrongs. One of them, as he departed, gave Nora a wink, as if to imply that the state of affairs between the two members of the firm was so broad a joke that even a pretty young woman might enjoy it. At last, when they had been alone again for half an hour, Mr. Franks closed with a slap the great leathern flanks of his account-book, and sat a moment burying his head in his arms. Then he suddenly rose and stood before the young girl. "Mr. Fenton's your cousin, Miss, you say, eh? Well, then let me tell you that your cousin's a swindler! I can prove it to you on those books! Nice books they are! Where is my money, thirty thousand dollars that I put into this d——d humbug of a business? What is there to show for it! I have been made a fool of,—as if I wasn't fool enough already." The tears stood in his eyes, he stamped with the bitterness of his spite; and then, thrusting his hat on his head and giving Nora's amazement no time to reply, he darted out of the door and went up the alley. Nora saw him from the window looking up and down the street. Suddenly, while he stood and while she looked, George came up. Mr. Franks's fury seemed suddenly to evaporate; he received his companion's hand-shake and nodded toward the office, as if to tell of Nora's being there; while, to her surprise, George hereupon, without looking toward the window, turned back into the street. In a few minutes, however, he reappeared alone, and in another moment he stood before her. "Well!" he cried; "here you are, then!"

"George," she said, "I have taken you at your word."

"My word? O yes!" cried George, bravely.

She saw that he was changed, and not for the better. He looked older, he was better dressed and more prosperous; but as Nora looked at him, she felt that she had asked too much of her imagination. He eyed her from head to foot, and in a moment he had noted her simple dress and her pale face. "What on earth has happened?" he asked, closing the door with a kick.

Nora hesitated, feeling that, with words, tears might come.

"You are sick," he said, "or you are going to be sick."

This horrible idea helped her to recall her self-control. "I have left Mr. Lawrence," she said.

"So I see!" said George, wavering between relish and disapproval. When, a few moments before, his partner had told him that a young lady was in the office, calling herself his cousin, he had straightway placed himself on his guard. The case was delicate; so that, instead of immediately advancing, he had retreated behind a green baize door twenty yards off, had "taken something," and briskly meditated. She had taken him at his word; he knew that before she told him. But confound his word if it came to this! It had been meant, not as an invitation to put herself under his care, but as a kind of speculative "feeler." Fenton, however, had a native sympathy with positive measures; and he felt, moreover, the instinct to angle in Nora's troubled waters. "What's the matter now?" he asked. "Have you quarrelled?"

"Don't call it a quarrel, George! He is as kind, he is kinder than ever," Nora cried. "But what do you think? He has asked me to marry him."

"Eh, my dear, I told you he would."

"I didn't believe you. I ought to have believed you. But it is not only that. It is that, years ago, he adopted me with that view. He brought me up for that purpose. He has done everything for me on that condition. I was to pay my debt and be his wife. I never dreamed of it. And now at last that I have grown up and he makes his claim, I can't, I can't!"

"You can't, eh? So you have left him!"

"Of course I have left him. It was the only thing to do. It was give and take. I cannot give what he wants, and I cannot give back what I have received. But I can refuse to take more."

Fenton sat on the edge of his desk, swinging his leg. He folded his arms and whistled a lively air, looking at Nora with a brightened eye. "I see, I see," he said.

Telling her tale had deepened her colour and added to her beauty. "So here I am," she went on. "I know that I am dreadfully alone, that I am homeless and helpless. But it's a heaven to living as I have lived. I have been content all these days, because I thought I could content him. But we never understood each other. He has given me immeasurable happiness; I know that; and he knows that I know it; don't you think he knows, George?" she cried, eager even in her reserve. "I would have made him a sister, a friend. But I don't expect you to understand all this. It's enough that I am satisfied. I am satisfied," the poor girl repeated vehemently. "I have no illusions about it now; you can trust me, George. I mean to earn my own living. I can teach; I am a good musician; I want above all things to work. I shall look for some employment without delay. All this time I might have been writing to Miss Murray. But I was sick with impatience to see you. To come to you was the only thing I could do; but I shall not trouble you for long."

Fenton seemed to have but half caught the meaning of this impassioned statement, for simple admiration of her exquisite purity of purpose was fast getting the better of his caution. He gave his knee a loud slap. "Nora," he said, "you're a wonderful young lady!"

For a moment she was silent and thoughtful. "For mercy's sake," she cried at last, "say nothing to make me feel that I have done this thing too easily, too proudly and recklessly! Really, I am anything but brave. I am full of doubts and fears."

"You're uncommonly handsome; that's one sure thing!" said Fenton. "I would rather marry you than lose you. Poor Mr. Lawrence!" Nora turned away in silence and walked to the window, which grew to her eyes, for the moment, as the "glimmering square" of the poet. "I thought you loved him so!" he added abruptly. Nora turned back with an effort and a blush. "If he were to come to you now," he went on, "and go down on his knees and beg and plead and rave and all that sort of thing, would you still refuse him?"

She covered her face with her hands. "O George, George!" she cried.

"He will follow you, of course. He will not let you go so easily."

"Possibly; but I have begged him solemnly to let me take my way. Roger is not one to rave and rage. At all events, I shall refuse to see him now. A year hence I will think of it. His great desire will be, of course, that I don't suffer. I shall not suffer."

"By Jove, not if I can help it!" cried Fenton, with warmth. Nora answered with a faint, grave smile, and stood looking at him in appealing silence. He coloured beneath her glance with the pressure of his thoughts.

They resolved themselves chiefly into the recurring question. "What can be made of it?" While he was awaiting inspiration, he took refuge in a somewhat inexpensive piece of gallantry. "By the way, you must be hungry."

"No, I am not hungry," said Nora, "but I am tired. You must find me a lodging,—in some quiet hotel."

"O, you shall be quiet enough," he answered; but he insisted that unless, meanwhile, she took some dinner, he should have her ill on his hands. They quitted the office, and he hailed a hack, which drove them over to the upper Broadway region, where they were soon established in a well-appointed restaurant. They made, however, no very hearty meal. Nora's hunger of the morning had passed away in fever, and Fenton himself was, as he would have expressed it, off his feed. Nora's head had begun to ache; she had removed her bonnet, and sat facing him at their small table, leaning wearily against the wall, her plate neglected, her arms folded, her bright expanded eyes consulting the uncertain future. He noted narrowly how much prettier she was; but more even than by her prettiness he was struck by her high spirit. This belonged to an order of things in which *he* felt no commission to dabble; but in a creature of another sort he was free to admire such a luxury of conscience. In man or woman the capacity then and there to *act* was the thing he most relished. Nora had not faltered and wavered; she had chosen, and here she sat. It was an irritation to him to feel that he was not the manner of man for whom such a girl would burn her ships; for, as he looked askance at her beautiful absent eyes, he more than suspected that there was a positive as well as a negative side to her refusal of her friend. Poor Roger had a happier counterpart. It was love and not indifference, that had pulled the wires of her adventure. Fenton, as we have intimated, was one who, when it suited him, could ride rough-shod to his mark. "You have told me half your story," he said, "but your eyes tell the rest. "You'll not be Roger's wife, but you'll not die an old maid."

Nora blushed, but she answered simply, "Please don't say that."

"My dear girl," he said, "I religiously respect your secrets." But, in truth, he only half respected them. Stirred as he was by her beauty and by that sense of feminine appealingness which may be an inspiring motive even to a very shabby fellow, he was keenly mortified by feeling that her tenderness passed him by, barely touching him with the hem of its garment. She was doing mighty fine things, but she was using him, her hard, vulgar cousin, as a senseless stepping-stone. These reflections quickened his appreciation of her charm, but took the edge from his delicacy. As they rose to go, Nora, who in spite of her absent eyes had watched him well, felt that cousinship had melted to a mere name. George had been to her maturer vision a painful disappointment. His face, from the moment of their meeting, had given her warning to withdraw her trust. Was it she or he who had changed since that fervid youthful parting of sixteen months before? She, in the interval, and been refined by life; he had been vulgarised. She had seen the world; she had known better things and better men; she had known Hubert, and, more than ever, she had known Roger. But as she drew on her gloves she reflected with horror that distress was making her fastidious. She wished to be coarse and careless; she wished that she might have eaten a heavy dinner, that she might enjoy taking George's arm. And the slower flowed the current of her confidence, the softer dropped her words. "Now, dear George," she said, with a desperate attempt at a cheerful smile, "let me know where you mean to take me."

"Upon my soul, Nora," he said, with a hard grin, "I feel as if I had a jewel I must lay in soft cotton. The thing is to find it soft enough." George himself, perhaps, she might endure; but she had a growing horror of his friends. Among them, probably, were the female correlatives of the "parties" who had come to chat with Mr. Franks. She prayed he might not treat her to company. "You see I want to do the pretty thing," he went on. "I want to treat you, by Jove, as I would treat a queen! I can't thrust you all alone into an hotel, and I can't put up at one with you,—can I?"

"I am not in a position to be fastidious," said Nora. "I shall not object to going alone."

"No, no!" he cried, with a flourish of his hand. "I will do for you what I would do for my own sister. I am not a fine gentleman, but I know what's proper. I live in the house of a lady who lets out rooms,—a very nice little woman; she and I are great cronies; I'm sure you'll like her. She will give you the comforts of a home, and all that sort of thing."

Nora's heart sank, but she assented. They re-entered

their carriage, and a drive of moderate length brought them to a brownstone dwelling of the third order of gentility, as one may say, stationed in a cheap and serried row. In a few moments, in a small tawdry front parlour, Nora was introduced to George's hostess, the nice little woman, Mrs. Paul by name. Nice enough she seemed, for Nora's comfort. She was young and fair, plump and comely; she wore a great many ringlets. She was a trifle too loving on short acquaintance, perhaps; but, after all, thought Nora, who was she now, to complain of that? When the two women had gone upstairs, Fenton put on his hat,—he could never meditate without it (he had written that last letter to Nora with his beaver resting on the bridge of his nose),—and paced slowly up and down the narrow entry, chewing the end of a cigar, with his hands in his pockets and his eyes on the ground. In ten minutes Mrs. Paul reappeared. "Well, sir," she cried, "what does all this mean?"

"It means money, if you'll not scream so loud," he answered. "Come in here." They went into the parlour and remained there for a couple of hours with closed doors. At last Fenton came forth and left the house. He walked along the street, humming·gently to himself. Dusk had fallen; he stopped beneath a lighted lamp at the corner, looked up and down a moment, and then exhaled a deep, an almost melancholy sigh. Having thus relieved his conscience, he proceeded to business. He consulted his watch; it was five o'clock. An empty hack rolled by; he called it and got in, breathing the motto of great spirits, "Confound the expense!" His business led him to visit successively several of the best hotels. Roger, he argued, starting immediately in pursuit of Nora, would have taken the first train from Boston, and would now have been more than an hour in town. Fenton could, of course, proceed only by probabilities; but according to these, Roger was to be found at one of the establishments I have mentioned. Fenton knew his New York, and, from what he knew of Roger, he believed him to be at the "quietest" of these. Here, in fact, he found his name freshly registered. He would give him time, however; he would take time himself. He stretched his long legs awhile on one of the divans in the hall. At last Roger appeared, strolling gloomily down the corridor, with his eyes on the ground. For a moment Fenton scarcely recognised him. He was pale and grave; distress had already made him haggard. Fenton observed that, as he passed, people stared at him. He walked slowly to the street door; whereupon Fenton, fearing he might lose him, followed him, and stood for a moment behind him. Roger turned suddenly, as if from an instinct of the other's nearness, and the two faced each other. Those dumb eyes of Roger's for once were eloquent. They glowed like living coals.

X

THE good lady who enjoyed the sinecure of being mother-in-law to Mrs. Keith passed on that especial Sunday an exceptionally dull evening. Her son's widow was oppressed and preoccupied, and took an early leave. Mrs. Keith's first question on reaching home was as to whether Nora had left her room. On learning that she had quitted the house alone, after dark, Mrs. Keith made her way, stirred by vague conjecture, to the empty chamber, where, of course, she speedily laid her hands on those two testamentary notes to which allusion has been made. In a moment she had read the one addressed to herself. Perturbed as she was, she yet could not repress an impulse of intelligent applause. "Ah, how character plays the cards!" she mused. "How a good girl's very errors set her off!" If Roger longed for Nora to-day, who could measure the morrow's longing? He might enjoy, however, without waiting for the morrow this refinement of desire. In spite of the late hour, Mrs. Keith repaired to his abode, armed with the other letter, deeming this, at such a moment, a more gracious course than to send for him. The letter Roger found to be brief but pregnant. "Dear Roger," it ran, "I learned this afternoon the secret of all these years,—too late for our happiness. I have been strangely blind; you have been too forbearing,—generous where you should have been strictly just. I never dreamed of what this day would bring. Now,

I must leave you; I can do nothing else. This is no time to thank you for what you have been to me, but I shall live to do so yet. Dear Roger, get married, and send me your children to teach. I shall live by teaching. I have a family, you know; I go to New York to-night. I write this on my knees, imploring you to be happy. One of these days, when I have learned to be myself again, we shall be better friends than ever. I beg you, I beg you, not to follow me."

Mrs. Keith sat a long time with her host. For the first time in her knowledge of him she saw Roger violent,— violent with horror and self-censure and vain impre-cation. "Take her at her word," she said; "don't follow her. Let her knock against the world a little, and she will have you yet."

This philosophy seemed to Roger too stoical by half; to sit at home and let Nora knock against the world was more than he could undertake. "Whether she will have me or not," he said, "I must bring her back. I am morally responsible for her. Good God! think of her afloat in that horrible city with that rascal of a half-cousin—her 'family' she calls him!—for a pilot!" He took, of course, the first train to New York. How to proceed, where to look, was a hard question; but to linger and waver was agony. He was haunted, as he went, with dreadful visions of what might have befallen her; it seemed to him that he had never loved her before.

Fenton, as he recognised him, was a comfortable sight, in spite of his detested identity. He was better than un-certainty. "You have news for me!" Roger cried. "Where is she?"

Fenton looked about him at his leisure, feeling, agreeably, that now *he* held the cards. "Gently," he said. "Hadn't we better retire?" Upon which Roger, grasping his arm with grim devotion, led him to his own apartment. "I rather hit it," George went on. "I am not the fool you once tried to make me seem."

"Where is she,—tell me that!" Roger repeated.

"Allow me, dear sir," said Fenton, settling himself in spacious vantage. "If I have come here to oblige you, you must let me take my own way. You don't suppose I have rushed to meet you for the pleasure of the thing. I owe it to my cousin, in the first place, to say that I have come without her knowledge."

"If you mean only to torture me," Roger answered, "say so outright. Is she well? is she safe?"

"Safe? the safest creature in the city, sir! A delightful home, maternal care!"

Roger wondered whether Fenton was making horrible sport of his trouble; he turned cold at the thought of maternal care of his providing. But he admonished himself to lose nothing by arrogance. "I thank you extremely for your kindness. Nothing remains but that I should see her."

"Nothing, indeed! You are very considerate. You know that she particularly objects to seeing you."

"Possibly! But that is for her to say. I claim the right to take the refusal from her own lips."

Fenton looked at him with an impudent parody of compassion. "Don't you think you have had refusals enough? You must enjoy them!"

Roger turned away with an imprecation, but he continued to swallow his impatience. "Mr. Fenton," he said, "you have not come here, I know, to waste words, nor have I to waste temper. You see before you a desperate man. Come, make the most of me! I am willing, I am delighted, to be fleeced! You will help me, but not for nothing. Name your terms."

Fenton flinched, but he did not protest; he only gave himself the luxury of swaggering a little. "Well, you see," he answered, "my assistance is worth something. Let me explain how much. You will never guess! I know your story; Nora has told me everything,—everything! We have had a great talk. Let me give you a little hint of my story,—and excuse egotism! You proposed to her; she refused you. You offered her money, luxury, a position. She knew you, she liked you enormously, yet she refused you flat! Now reflect on this."

There was something revolting to Roger in seeing his adversary profaning these sacred mysteries; he protested. "I *have* reflected, quite enough. You can tell me nothing. Her affections," he added stiffly, to make an end of it, "were pre-engaged."

"Exactly! You see how that complicates matters. Poor, dear little Nora!" And Fenton gave a twist to his moustache. "Imagine, if you can, how a man placed as I am feels toward a woman,—toward *the* woman! If he reciprocates, it's love, it's passion, it's what you will, but it's common enough! But when he doesn't repay her in kind, when he can't poor devil, it's—it's—upon my word," cried Fenton, slapping his knee, "it's chivalry!"

For some moments Roger failed to appreciate the remarkable purport of these observations; then suddenly, it dawned upon him. "Do I understand you," he asked in a voice gentle by force of wonder, "that *you* are the man?"

Fenton squared himself in his chair. "You have hit it, sir. I am the man,—the happy, the unhappy man. D——n it, sir, it's not my fault!"

Roger stood staring; Fenton felt his eyes penetrating him to the core. "Excuse me," said Roger, at last, "if I suggest your giving me some slight evidence in support of this extraordinary claim!"

"Evidence? isn't there about evidence enough? When a young girl gives up home and friends and fortune and —and reputation, and rushes out into the world to throw herself into a man's arms, it seems to me you have got your evidence. But if you'll not take my word, you may leave it! I may look at the matter once too often, let me tell you! I admire Nora with all my heart; I worship the ground she treads on; but I confess I'm afraid of her; she's too good for me; she was meant for a finer gentleman than I! By which I don't mean *you*, of necessity. But you have been good to her, and you have a claim. It has been cancelled in a measure; but you wish to set it up again. Now you see that I stand in your way; that if I had a mind to, I might stand there for ever! Hang it, sir, I am playing the part of a saint. I have but a word to say to settle my case, and to settle yours. But I have my eye on a lady neither so young nor so pretty as my cousin, yet whom I can marry with a better conscience, for she expects no more than I can give her. Nevertheless, I don't answer for myself. A man isn't a saint every day in the week. Talk about conscience when a beautiful girl sits gazing at you through a mist of tears! O, you have yourself to thank for it all! A year and a half ago, if you hadn't treated me like a swindler, Nora would have been content to treat me like a friend. But women have a fancy for an outlaw. You turned me out of doors, and Nora's heart went with me. It has followed me ever since. Here I sit with my ugly face and hold it in my hand. As I say, I don't quite know what to do with it. You propose an arrangement, I inquire your terms. A man loved is a man listened to. If I were to say to Nora to-morrow, 'My dear girl, you have made a mistake. You are in a false position. Go back to Mr. Lawrence directly, and then we will talk about it!' she would look at me a moment with those beautiful eyes of hers, she would sigh, she would gather herself up like a princess on trial for treason, remanded to prison,—and she would march to your door. Once she's within it, it's your own affair. That's what I can do. Now what can you do? Come, something handsome!"

Fenton spoke loud and fast, as if to outstrip self-contempt. Roger listened amazedly to this tissue of falsity, impudence, and greed, and at last, as Fenton paused, and he seemed to see Nora's very image turning away with a shudder, his disgust broke forth. "Upon my word, sir," he cried, "you go too far; you ask too much. Nora in love with you,—you, who haven't the grace even to lie decently! Tell me she's ill, she's lost, she's dead; but don't tell me she can look at you without horror!"

Fenton rose and stood for a moment, glaring with anger at his useless self-exposure. For an instant, Roger expected a tussle. But Fenton deemed that he could deal harder vengeance than by his fists. "Very good!" he cried. "You have chosen. I don't mind your words; you're an ass at best, and of course you are twenty times an ass when you are put out by a disagreeable truth. But you are not such a fool, I guess, as not to repent!" And Fenton made a rather braver exit than you might have expected.

Roger's recent vigil with Mrs. Keith had been dismal enough; but he was yet to learn that a sleepless night may contain deeper possibilities of suffering. He had flung back Fenton's words, but they returned to the charge. When once the gate is opened to self-torture, the whole army of fiends files in. Before morning he had fairly out-Fentoned Fenton. There was no discretion in his own love; why should there be in Nora's? We love as we must, not as we should; and she, poor girl, might have bowed to the common law. In the morning he slept awhile for weariness, but he awoke to a world of agitation. If Fenton's tale was true, and if, at Mrs. Keith's instigation, his own suspicions had done Hubert wrong, he would go to Hubert, pour out his woes, and demand aid and comfort. He must move to find rest. Hubert's lodging was far up town; Roger started on foot. The weather was perfect; one of those happy days of February which seem to snatch a mood from May,—a day when any sorrow is twice a sorrow. The winter was melting and trickling; you heard on all sides, in the still sunshine, the raising of windows; on the edges of opposing house-tops rested a vault of vernal blue. Where was she hidden, in the vast bright city? The streets and crowds and houses that concealed her seemed hideous. He would have beggared himself for the sound of her voice, though her words might damn him. When at last he reached Hubert's dwelling, a sudden sense of all that he risked checked his steps. Hubert, after all, and Hubert alone, was a possible rival, and it would be sad work to put the torch into his hands! So he turned heavily back to the Fifth Avenue and kept his way to the Park. Here for some time he walked about, heeding, feeling, seeing nothing but the glaring, mocking brightness of the day. At last he sat down on a bench; the delicious mildness of the air almost sickened him. It was some time before he perceived through the mist of his thoughts that two ladies had descended from a carriage hard by, and were approaching his bench,—the only one near at hand. One of these ladies was of great age and evidently infirm; she came slowly, leaning on her companion's arm; she wore a green shade over her eyes. The younger lady, who was in the prime of youth and beauty, supported her friend with peculiar tenderness. As Roger rose to give them place, he dimly observed on the young lady's face a movement of recognition, a smile,—the smile of Miss Sands! Blushing slightly, she frankly greeted him. He met her with the best grace at his command, and felt her eyes, as he spoke, scanning the trouble in his aspect. "There is no need of my introducing you to my aunt," she said. "She has lost her hearing, and her only pleasure is to bask in the sun." She turned and helped this venerable invalid to settle herself on the bench, put a shawl about her, and satisfied her feeble needs with filial solicitude. At the end of ten minutes of common-place talk, relieved however by certain intelligent glances on either side, Roger found a kind of healing quality in the presence of this agreeable woman. At last these sympathetic eyebeams resolved themselves, on Miss Sands's part, into speech. "You are either very unwell, Mr. Lawrence, or very unhappy."

Roger hesitated an instant, under the empire of that stubborn aversion to complaint which, in his character, was half modesty and half philosophy. But Miss Sands seemed to sit there eyeing him so like the genius of friendship, that he answered simply, "I am unhappy!"

"I was afraid it would come!" said Miss Sands. "It seemed to me when we met, a year ago, that your spirits were too high for this life. You know you told me something which gives me the right,—I was going to say, to be interested; let me say, at least, to be compassionate."

"I hardly remember what I told you. I only know that I admired you to a degree which may very well have loosened my tongue."

"O, it was about the charms of another you spoke! You told me about the young girl to whom you had devoted yourself."

"I was dreaming then; now I am awake!" Roger hung his head and poked the ground with his stick. Suddenly he looked up, and she saw that his eyes were filled with tears. "Dear lady," he said, "you have stirred deep waters! Don't question me. I am ridiculous with dis-appointment and sorrow!"

She gently laid her hand upon his arm. "Let me hear it all! I assure you I can't go away and leave you sitting here the same image of suicidal despair I found you."

Thus urged, Roger told his story. Her attention made him understand it better himself, and, as he talked, he worked off the superficial disorder of his grief. When he came to speak of this dismal contingency of Nora's love for her cousin, he threw himself frankly upon Miss Sands's pity, upon her wisdom. "Is such a thing possible?" he asked. "Do you believe it?"

She raised her eyebrows. "You must remember that I know neither Miss Lambert nor the gentleman you speak of. I can hardly risk a judgement; I can only say this, that the general effect of your story is to diminish my esteem for women,—to elevate my opinion of men."

"O, except Nora on one side, and Fenton on the other! Nora is an angel!"

Miss Sands gave a vexed smile. "Possibly! You are a man, and you ought to have loved a woman. Angels have a good conscience guaranteed them; they may do what they please. If I should except any one, it would be Mr. Hubert Lawrence. I met him the other evening."

"You think it is Hubert, then?" Roger demanded mournfully.

Miss Sands broke into a brilliant laugh. "For an angel, Miss Lambert hasn't lost her time on earth! But don't ask me for advice, Mr. Lawrence; at least not now and here. Come and see me to-morrow, or this evening. Don't regret having spoken; you may believe at least that the burden of your grief is shared. It was too miserable that at such a time you should be sitting here alone, feeding upon your own heart."

These seemed to Roger excellent words; they lost nothing on the speaker's lips. She was indeed extremely beautiful; her face, softened by intelligent pity, was lighted by a gleam of tender irony of his patience. Was he, after all, stupidly patient, ignobly fond? There was in Miss Sands something delightfully rich and mellow. Nora, for an instant, seemed a flighty school-girl. He looked about him, vaguely questioning the empty air, longing for rest, yet dreading forfeiture. He left his place and strolled across the dull-coloured turf. At the base of a tree, on its little bed of sparse raw verdure, he suddenly spied the first violet of the year. He stooped and picked it; its mild firm tint was the colour of friendship. He brought it back to Miss Sands, who now had risen with her companion and was preparing to return to the carriage. He silently offered her the violet,—a mere pin's head of bloom; a passionate throb of his heart had told him that this was all he could offer her. She took it with a sober smile; it seemed to grow pale beneath her dark blue eyes. "We shall see you again?" she said.

Roger felt himself blushing to his brows. He had a vision on either hand of an offered cup,—the deep-hued wine of illusion,—the bitter draught of constancy. A certain passionate instinct answered,—an instinct deeper than his wisdom, his reason, his virtue,—deep as his love. "Not now," he said. "A year hence!"

Miss Sands turned away and stood for a moment as motionless as some sculptured statue of renunciation. Then, passing her arm caressingly round her companion. "Come, dear aunt," she murmured; "we must go." This little address to the stone-deaf dame was her single tribute to confusion. Roger walked with the ladies to their carriage and silently helped them to enter it. He noted the affectionate tact with which Miss Sands adjusted her movements to those of her companion. When he lifted his hat, his friend bowed, as he fancied, with an air of redoubled compassion. She had but imagined his prior loss,—she knew his present one! "She would make an excellent wife!" he said, as the carriage rolled away. He stood watching it for some minutes; then, as it wheeled round a turn, he was seized with a deeper, sorer sense of his impotent idleness. He would go to Hubert with his accusation, if not with his appeal.

XI

NORA, relieved of her hostess's company, turned the key
in her door and went through certain motions mechanically suggestive of her being at rest and satisfied. She un-
packed her little bag and repaired her disordered toilet.
She took out her inkstand and prepared to write a letter
to Miss Murray. But she had not written many words
before she lapsed into sombre thought. Now that she had
seen George again and judged him, she was coming
rapidly to feel that to have exchanged Roger's care for
his care was, for the time, to have paid a scanty compliment to Roger. But she took refuge from this reflexion
in her letter, and begged for an immediate reply. From
time to time, as she wrote, she heard a step in the house
which she supposed to be George's; it somehow quickened her pen and the ardour of her petition. This was
just finished when Mrs. Paul reappeared, bearing a salver
charged with tea and toast,—a gracious attention, which
Nora was unable to repudiate. The lady took advantage
of it to open a conversation. Mrs. Paul's overtures, as
well as her tea and toast, were the result of her close con-
ference with Fenton; but though his instructions had
made a very pretty show as he laid them down, they
dwindled sensibly in the vivid glare of Nora's mistrust.
Mrs. Paul, nevertheless, seated herself bravely on the bed
and rubbed her plump pretty hands like the best little
woman in the world. But the more Nora looked at her,

the less she liked her. At the end of five minutes she had conceived a horror of her comely stony face, her false smile, her little tulle cap, her artificial ringlets. Mrs. Paul called her my dear, and tried to take her hand; Nora was afraid that, the next thing, she would kiss her. With a defiant flourish, Nora addressed her letter with Miss Murray's venerated title; "I should like to have this posted, please," she said.

"Give it to me, my dear; I will attend to it," said Mrs. Paul; and straightway read the address. "I suppose this is your old schoolmistress. Mr. Fenton told me all about it." Then, after turning the letter for a moment, "Keep it over a day!"

"Not an hour," said Nora, with decision. "My time is precious."

"Why, my dear," said Mrs. Paul, "we shall be delighted to keep you a month."

"You are very good. You know I have my living to make."

"Don't talk about that! I make *my* living,—I know what it means! Come, let me talk to you as a friend. Don't go too far. Suppose, now, you take it all back? Six months hence, it may be too late. If you leave him lamenting too long, he'll marry the first pretty girl he sees. They always do,—a man refused is just like a widower. They're not so faithful as the widows! But let me tell you it's not every girl that gets such a chance; I would have snapped at it. He'll love you the better, you see, for your having led him a little dance. But he mustn't dance too long! Excuse the liberty I take; but Mr. Fenton and I, you see, are great friends, and I feel as if his cousin was my cousin. Take back this letter and give me just one word to post, —*Come!* Poor little man! You must have a high opinion of men, my dear, to play such a game with this one!"

If Roger had wished for a proof that Nora still cared for him, he would have found it in the disgust she felt at hearing Mrs. Paul undertake his case. The young girl coloured with her sense of the defilement of sacred things. George, surely, for an hour, at least, might have kept her story intact. "Really, madam," she answered, "I can't discuss this matter. I am extremely obliged to you." But Mrs. Paul was not to be so easily baffled. Poor Roger, roaming helpless and hopeless, would have been amazed to hear how warmly his cause was being urged. Nora, of course, made no attempt to argue the case. She waited till the lady had exhausted her eloquence, and then, "I am a very obstinate person," she said; "you waste your words. If you go any further I shall take offence." And she rose, to signify that Mrs. Paul might do likewise. Mrs. Paul took the hint, but in an instant she had turned about the hard reverse of her fair face, in which defeated self-interest smirked horribly. "Bah! you're a silly girl!" she cried, and swept out of the room. Nora, after this, determined to avoid a second interview with George. Her bad headache furnished a sufficient pretext for escaping it. Half an hour later he knocked at her door; quite too loudly, she thought, for good taste. When she opened it, he stood there, excited, angry, ill-disposed. "I am sorry you are ill," he said; "but a night's rest will put you right. I have seen Roger."

"Roger! is he here?"

"Yes, he's here. But he don't know where you are. Thank the Lord you left him! he's a brute!" Nora would fain have learned more,—whether he was angry, whether he was suffering, whether he had asked to see her; but at these words she shut the door in her cousin's face. She hardly dared think of what offered impertinence this outbreak of Fenton's was the rebound. Her night's rest brought little comfort. She wondered whether Roger had supposed George to be her appointed mediator, and asked herself whether it was not her duty to see him once again and bid him a respectfully personal farewell. It was a long time after she rose before she could bring herself to leave her room. She had a vague hope that if she delayed, her companions might have gone out. But in the dining-room, in spite of the late hour, she found George gallantly awaiting her. He had apparently had the discretion to dismiss Mrs. Paul to the background, and apologised for her absence by saying that she had breakfasted long since and had left the house. He seemed to have slept off his wrath and was full of brotherly *bonhomie*. "I suppose you will want to know about Roger," he said, when they were seated at breakfast. "He had followed you directly, in spite of your hope that he wouldn't; but it was not to beg you to come back. He counts on your repentance, and he expects you to break down and come to him on your knees, to beg his pardon and promise never to do it again. Pretty terms to marry a man on, for a woman of spirit! But he doesn't know his woman, does he, Nora? Do you know what he intimated? indeed, he came right out with it. That you and I want to make a match! That you're in love with me, Miss, and ran away to marry me. That we expected him to forgive us and endow us with a pile of money. But he'll not forgive us,—not he! We may starve, we and our brats, before he looks at us. Much obliged. We shall thrive, for many a year, as brother and sister, sha'n't we, Nora, and need neither his money nor his pardon?"

In reply to this speech, Nora sat staring in pale amazement. "Roger thought," she at last found words to say, "that it was to marry *you* I refused him,—to marry *you* I came to New York?"

Fenton, with seven-and-twenty years of impudence at his back, had received in his day snubs and shocks of various shades of intensity; but he had never felt in his face so chilling a blast of reprobation as this cold disgust of Nora's. We know that the scorn of a lovely woman makes cowards brave; it may do something towards making knaves honest men. "Upon my word, my dear," he cried, "I am sorry I hurt your feelings. It may be offensive, but it is true."

Nora wished in after years she had been able to laugh at this disclosure; to pretend, at least, to an exhilaration she so little felt. But she remained almost sternly silent, with her eyes on her plate, stirring her tea. Roger, meanwhile, was walking about under this detestable deception. Let him think anything but that! "What did you reply," she asked, "to this—to this——"

"To this handsome compliment? I replied that I only wished it were true; but that I feared I had no such luck!

Upon which he told me to go to the Devil,—in a tone which implied that he didn't much care if you went with me."

Nora listened to this speech in freezing silence. "Where is Roger?" she asked at last.

Fenton shot her a glance of harsh mistrust. "Where is he? What do you want to know that for?"

"Where is he, please?" she simply repeated. And then, suddenly, she wondered how and where it was the two men had happened to meet. "Where did you find him?" she went on. "How did it happen?"

Fenton drained his cup of tea at one long gulp before he answered. "My dear Nora," he said, "it's all very well to be modest, it's all very well to be proud; but take care you are not ungrateful! I went purposely to look him up. I was convinced he would have followed you to beg and implore you, as I supposed, to come back. I wanted to say to him, 'She's safe, she's happy, she's in the best hands. Don't waste your time, your words, your hopes. Give her rope. Go quietly home and leave things to me. If she gets homesick, I will let you know.' You see I'm frank, Nora; that's what I meant to say. But I was received with this broadside. I found a perfect bluster of injured vanity. 'You're her lover, she's your mistress, and be d——d to both of you!'"

That George deliberately lied Nora did not distinctly say to herself, for she lacked practice in this range of incrimination. But she as little said to herself that this could be the truth. "I am not ungrateful," she answered firmly "But where was it?"

At this, George pushed back his chair. "Where—

where? Don't you believe me? Do you want to go and ask him if it's true? What is the matter with you, anyway? What are you up to? Have you put yourself into my hands, or not?" A certain manly indignation was now kindled in his breast; he was equally angry with Roger, with Nora, and with himself; fate had offered him an overdose of contumely, and he felt a reckless, savage impulse to wring from the occasion that compliment to his power which had been so rudely denied to his delicacy. "Are you using me simply as a vulgar tool? Don't you care for me the least little bit? Let me suggest that for a girl in your—your ambiguous position, you are several shades too proud. Don't go back to Roger in a hurry! You are not the immaculate young person you were but two short days ago. Who am I, what am I, to the people whose opinion you care for? A very low fellow, my dear; and yet, in the eyes of the world, you have certainly taken up with me. If you are not prepared to do more, you should have done less. Nora, Nora," he went on, breaking into a vein none the less revolting for being more ardent, "I confess I don't understand you! But the more you puzzle me the more you fascinate me; and the less you like me the more I love you. What has there been, anyway, between you and Lawrence? Hang me if I can understand! Are you an angel of purity, or are you the most audacious of flirts?"

She had risen before he had gone far. "Spare me," she said, "the necessity of hearing your opinions or answering your questions. Please be a gentleman! Tell me, I once more beg of you, where Roger is to be found?"

"Be a gentleman!" was a galling touch. He placed himself before the door. "I refuse the information," he said. "I don't mean to have been played with, to have been buffeted hither by Roger and thither by you! I mean to make something out of all this. I mean to request you to remain quietly in this room. Mrs. Paul will keep you company. You didn't treat her over well, yesterday; but, in her way, she is quite as strong as you. Meanwhile I shall go to our friend. 'She's locked up tight,' I will say; 'she's as good as in jail. Give me five thousand dollars and I'll let her out.' Of course he will begin to talk about legal proceedings. Then I will tell him that he is welcome to take legal proceedings if he doesn't mind the exposure. The exposure won't be pleasant for you, Nora, you know; for the public takes things in the lump. It won't hurt me!"

"Heaven forgive you!" murmured Nora, for all response to this explosion. It made a hideous whirl about her; but she felt that to advance in the face of it was her best safety. It sickened rather than frightened her. She went to the door. "Let me pass!" she said.

Fenton stood motionless, leaning his head against the door, with his eyes closed. She faced him a moment, looking at him intently. He seemed ineffably repulsive. "Coward!" she cried. He opened his eyes at the sound; for an instant they met hers; then a burning blush blazed out strangely on his dead complexion; he strode past her, dropped into a chair, and buried his face in his hands. "O Lord!" he cried. "I am an ass!"

Nora made it the work of a single moment to reach her own room and fling on her bonnet and shawl, of another

227

to descend to the hall door. Once in the street she never stopped running till she had turned a corner and put the house out of sight. She went far, hurried along by the ecstasy of relief and escape, and it was some time before she perceived that this was but half the question, and that she was now quite without refuge. Thrusting her hand into her pocket to feel for her purse, she found that she had left it in her room. Stunned and sickened as she was already, it can hardly be said that the discovery added to her grief. She was being precipitated toward a great decision; sooner or later made little difference. The thought of seeing Hubert Lawrence had now taken possession of her. Reserve, prudence, mistrust, had melted away; she was mindful only of her trouble, of his nearness, and of the way he had once talked to her. His address she well remembered, and she neither paused nor faltered. To say even that she reflected would be to speak amiss, for her longing and her haste were one. Between them both it was with a beating heart that she reached his door. The servant admitted her without visible surprise (for Nora wore, as she conceived, the air of some needy parishioner) and ushered her into his bachelor's parlour. As she crossed the threshold, she perceived with something both of regret and of relief that he was not alone. He was sitting somewhat stiffly, with folded arms, facing the window, near which, before an easel, stood a long-haired gentleman of foreign and artistic aspect, giving the finishing touches to a portrait in crayons. Hubert was in position for a likeness of his handsome face. When Nora appeared, his handsome face remained for a moment a blank; the next it turned most eloquently pale. "Miss Lambert!" he cried.

There was such a tremor in his voice that Nora felt that, for the moment, she must have self-possession for both. "I interrupt you," she said with extreme deference.

"We are just finishing!" Hubert answered. "It is my portrait, you see. You must look at it." The artist made way for her before the easel, laid down his implements, and took up his hat and gloves. She looked mechanically at the picture, while Hubert accompanied him to the door, and they talked awhile about another sitting, and about a frame that was to be sent home. The portrait was clever, but superficial; better looking, at once, and worse looking than Hubert,—elegant, effeminate, unreal. An impulse of wonder passed through her mind that she should happen just then to find him engaged in this odd self-reproduction. It was a different Hubert that turned and faced her as the door closed behind his companion, the real, the familiar Hubert. He had gained time; but surprise, admiration, conjecture, a lively suggestion of dismay, were shining in his handsome eyes. Nora had dropped into the chair vacated by the artist; and as she sat there with clasped hands, she felt the young man reading the riddle of her shabby dress and her excited face. For him, too, she was the real Nora. Dismay in Hubert's face began to elbow its companions. He advanced, pushed towards her the chair in which he had been posturing, and, as he seated himself, made a half-movement to offer his hand; but before she could take it, he had begun to play with his watch-chain. "Nora," he asked, "what is it?"

What was it, indeed? What was her errand, and in what words could it be told? An inexpressible weakness had taken possession of her, a sense of having reached the goal of her journey, the term of her strength. She dropped her eyes on her shabby skirt and passed her hand over it with a gesture of eloquent simplicity. "I have left Roger," she said.

Hubert made no answer, but his silence seemed to fill the room. He sank back in his chair, still looking at her with startled eyes. The fact intimidated him; he was amazed and confused; yet he felt he must say something, and in his confusion he uttered a gross absurdity. "Ah," he said; "with his consent?"

The sound of his voice was so grateful to her that, at first, she hardly heeded his words. "I am alone," she added, "I am free." It was after she had spoken, as she saw him, growing, to his own sense, infinitely small in the large confidence of her gaze, rise in a kind of agony of indecision and stand before her, stupidly staring, that she felt he had neither taken her hand, nor dropped at her feet, nor divinely guessed her trouble; that, in fact, his very silence was a summons to tell her story and justify herself. Her presence there was either a rapture or a shame. Nora felt as if she had taken a jump, and was learning in mid-air that the distance was tenfold what she had imagined. It is strange how the hinging-point of great emotions may rest on an instant of time. These instants, however, seem as ages, viewed from within; and in such a reverberating moment Nora felt something that she had believed to be a passion melting from beneath her feet, crumbling and crashing into the gulf on whose edge she stood. But her shame at least should be brief. She rose and bridged this dizzy chasm with some tragic counterfeit of a smile. "I have come—I have come——" She began and faltered. It was a pity some great actress had not been there to note upon the tablets of her art the light, all-eloquent tremor of tone with which she transposed her embarrassment into the petition, "Could you lend me a little money?"

Hubert was simply afraid of her. All his falsity, all his levity, all his egotism and sophism, seemed to crowd upon him and accuse him in deafening chorus; he seemed exposed and dishonoured. It was with an immense sense of relief that he heard her ask this simple favour. Money? Would money buy his release? He took out his purse and grasped a roll of bills; then suddenly he was overwhelmed by a sense of his cruelty. He flung the thing on the floor, and passed his hands over his face. "Nora, Nora," he cried, "say it outright; you despise me!"

He had become, in the brief space of a moment, the man she once had loved; but if he was no longer the rose, he stood too near it to be wantonly bruised. Men and women alike need in some degree to respect those they have suffered to wrong them. She stooped and picked up the porte-monnaie, like a beggar-maid in a ballad. "A very little will do," she said. "In a day or two I hope to be independent."

"Tell me at least what has happened!" he cried.

She hesitated a moment. "Roger has asked me to be his wife." Hubert's head swam with the vision of all that this simple statement embodied and implied. "I refused," Nora added, "and, having refused, I was unwilling to live any longer on his—on his——" Her speech at the last word melted into silence, and she seemed to fall a-musing. But in an instant she recovered herself. "I remember your once saying that you would have liked to see me poor and homeless. Here I am! You ought at least," she added with a laugh, "to pay for the exhibition!"

Hubert abruptly drew out his watch. "I expect here at any moment," he said, "a young lady of whom you may have heard. She is to come and see my portrait. I am engaged to marry her. I was engaged to marry her five months ago. She is rich, pretty, charming. Say but a single word, that you don't despise me, that you forgive me, and I will give her up, now, here, for ever, and be anything you will take me for,—your husband, your friend, your slave!" To have been able to make this speech gave Hubert immense relief. He felt almost himself again.

Nora fixed her eyes on him, with a kind of unfathomable gentleness. "You are engaged, you *were* engaged? How strangely you talk about giving her up! Give her my compliments!" It seemed, however, that Nora was to have the chance of offering her compliments personally. The door was thrown open and admitted two ladies whom Nora vaguely remembered to have seen. In a moment she recognised them as the persons whom, on the evening she had gone to hear Hubert preach, he had left her, after the sermon, to conduct to their carriage. The younger one was decidedly pretty, in spite of a nose a trifle too aquiline. A pair of imperious dark eyes, as bright as the diamond which glittered in each of her ears, and a nervous, capricious rapidity of motion and gesture, gave her an air of girlish *brusquerie* which was by no means without charm. Her mother's aspect, however, testified to its being as well to enjoy this charm at a distance. She was a stout, coarse-featured, good-natured woman, with a jaded, submissive expression, and seemed to proclaim by a certain ponderous docility, as she followed in her daughter's wake, the subserviency of matter to mind. Both ladies were dressed to the uttermost limit of opportunity. They came into the room staring frankly at Nora, and overlooking Hubert, with a gracious implication of his being already one of the family. The situation was a trying one, but he faced it as he might.

"This is Miss Lambert," he said gravely; and then with an effort to dissipate embarrassment by a jest, waving his hand toward his portrait, "This is the Reverend Hubert Lawrence!"

The elder lady moved toward the picture, but the other came straight to Nora. "I have seen you before!" she cried defiantly, and with defiance in her pretty eyes. "And I have heard of you too! Yes, you are certainly very handsome. But pray, what are you doing here?"

"My dear child!" said Hubert imploringly, and with a burning side-glance at Nora. The world seemed to him certainly very cruel.

"My dear Hubert," said the young lady, "what is she doing here? I have a right to know. Have you come running after him even here? You are a wicked girl. You have done me a wrong. You have tried to turn him away from me. You kept him in Boston for weeks, when he ought to have been here; when I was writing to him day after day to come. I heard all about it! I don't know what is the matter with you. I thought you were so very well off! You look very poor and unhappy, but I must say what I think!"

"My own darling, be reasonable!" murmured her mother. "Come and look at this beautiful picture. There's no deceit in that noble face!"

Nora smiled charitably. "Don't attack me," she said. "If I ever wronged you, I was quite unconscious of it, and I beg your pardon now."

"Nora," murmured Hubert piteously, "spare me!"

"Ah, does he call you Nora?" cried the young lady. "The harm's done, madam! He will never be what he was. You have changed, Hubert!" And she turned passionately upon her intended. "You know you have! You talk to me, but you think of her. And what is the meaning of this visit? You are both strangely excited; what have you been talking about?"

"Mr. Lawrence has been telling me about you," said Nora; "how pretty, how charming, how gentle you are!"

"I am not gentle!" cried the other. "You are laughing at me! Was it to talk about my prettiness you came here? Do you go about alone, this way? I never heard of such a thing. You are shameless! do you know that? But I am very glad of it; because once you have done this for him, he will not care for you. That's the way with men. And

I am not pretty either, not as you are! You are pale and tired; you have got a horrid dress and shawl, and yet you are beautiful! Is that the way I must look to please you?" she demanded, turning back to Hubert.

Hubert, during this rancorous tirade, had stood looking as dark as thunder, and at this point he broke out fiercely, "Good God, Amy! hold your tongue,—I command you."

Nora, gathering her shawl together, gave Hubert a glance. "She loves you," she said softly.

Amy stared a moment at this vehement adjuration; then she melted into a smile and turned in ecstasy to her mother. "O, did you hear that?" she cried. "That's how I like him. Please say it again!"

Nora left the room; and, in spite of her gesture of earnest deprecation, Hubert followed her downstairs to the street. "Where are you going?" he asked in a whisper. "With whom are you staying?"

"I am alone," said Nora.

"Alone in this great city? Nora, I *will* do something for you."

"Hubert," she said, "I never in my life needed help less than at this moment. Farewell." He fancied for an instant that she was going to offer him her hand, but she only motioned him to open the door. He did so, and she passed out.

She stood there on the pavement, strangely, almost absurdly, free and light of spirit. She knew neither whither she should turn nor what she should do, yet the fears which had haunted her for a whole day and

235

night had vanished. The sky was blazing blue overhead; the opposite side of the street was all in sun; she hailed the joyous brightness of the day with a kind of answering joy. She seemed to be in the secret of the universe. A nursery-maid came along, pushing a baby in a perambulator. She stooped and greeted the child, and talked pretty nonsense to it with a fervour which left the young woman staring. Nurse and child went their way, and Nora lingered, looking up and down the empty street. Suddenly a gentleman turned into it from the cross-street above. He was walking fast; he had his hat in his hand, and with his other hand he was passing his handkerchief over his forehead. As she stood and watched him draw near, down the bright vista of the street, there came upon her a singular and altogether nameless sensation, strangely similar to the one she had felt a couple of years before, when a physician had given her a dose of ether. The gentleman, she perceived was Roger; but the short interval of space and time which separated them seemed to expand into a throbbing immensity and eternity. She seemed to be watching him for an age, and, as she did so, to be floating through the whole circle of emotion and the full realisation of being. Yes, she was in the secret of the universe, and the secret of the universe was, that Roger was the only man in it who had a heart. Suddenly she felt a palpable grasp. Roger stood before her, and had taken her hand. For a moment he said nothing; but the touch of his hand spoke loud. They stood for an instant scanning the change in each other's faces. "Where are you going?" said Roger at last, imploringly.

Nora read silently in his haggard eyes the whole record of his suffering. It is a strange truth that this seemed the most beautiful thing she had ever looked upon; the sight of it was delicious. It seemed to whisper louder and louder that secret about Roger's heart.

Nora collected herself as solemnly as one on a death-bed making a will; but Roger was still in miserable doubt and dread. "I have followed you," he said, "in spite of that request in your letter."

"Have you got my letter?" Nora asked.

"It was the only thing you had left me," he said, and drew it forth, creased and crumpled.

She took it from him and thrust it into the pocket of her dress, never taking her eyes off his own. "Don't try and forget that I wrote it," she said. "I want you to see me burn it up, and to remember that."

"What does it mean, Nora?" he asked, in hardly audible tones.

"It means that I am a wiser girl to-day than *then*. I know myself better, I know you better. O Roger!" she cried, "it means everything!"

He passed her hand through his arm and held it there against his heart, while he stood looking hard at the pavement, as if to steady himself amid this great convulsion of things. Then raising his head, "Come," he said; "come!"

But she detained him, laying her other hand on his arm. "No; you must understand first. If I am wiser now, I have learnt wisdom at my cost. I am not the girl you proposed to on Sunday. I feel—I feel *dishonoured*!"

she said, uttering the word with a vehemence that stirred his soul to its depths.

"My own poor child!" he murmured, staring.

"There is a young girl in that house," Nora went on, "who will tell you that I am shameless!"

"What house? what young girl?"

"I don't know her name. Hubert is engaged to marry her."

Roger gave a glance at the house behind them, as if to fling defiance and oblivion upon all that it suggested and contained. Then turning to Nora with a smile of exquisite tenderness: "My dear Nora, what have *we* to do with Hubert's young girls?"

Roger, the reader will admit, was on a level with the occasion,—as with every other occasion that subsequently presented itself.

Mrs. Keith and Mrs. Lawrence are very good friends. On being complimented on possessing the confidence of so charming a woman as Mrs. Lawrence, Mrs. Keith has been known to say, opening and shutting her fan, "The fact is, Nora is under a very peculiar obligation to me!"

Selected Grove Press Paperbacks

B3	HODEIR, ANDRE / Jazz: Its Evolution and Essence / $2.95
E456	IONESCO, EUGENE / Exit the King / $2.95
E101	IONESCO, EUGENE / Four Plays (The Bald Soprano, The Lesson, The Chairs, and Jack or The Submission) / $2.95
E573	KEENE, DONALD, ed. / Modern Japanese Literature / $7.95
E522	KEROUAC, JACK / Mexico City Blues / $3.95
B9	LAWRENCE, D. H. / Lady Chatterley's Lover / $1.95
B373	LUCAS, GEORGE / American Graffiti / $2.95
B146	MALCOLM X / The Autobiography of Malcolm X / $1.95
E716	MAMET, DAVID / The Water Engine and Mr. Happiness / $3.95
B10	MILLER, HENRY / Tropic of Cancer / $1.95
B59	MILLER, HENRY / Tropic of Capricorn / $1.95
E636	NERUDA, PABLO / Five Decades: Poems 1925–1970. Bilingual ed. / $5.95
E687	OE, KENZABURO / Teach Us To Outgrow Our Madness / $4.95
E315	PINTER, HAROLD / The Birthday Party and The Room / $2.95
E411	PINTER, HAROLD / The Homecoming / $1.95
GP411	REAGE, PAULINE / Story of O. Illustrated by Guido Crepax / $7.95
B213	RECHY, JOHN / City of Night / $1.95
B69	ROBBE-GRILLET, ALAIN / Two Novels: Jealousy and In the Labyrinth / $4.95
B138	SADE, MARQUIS DE / The 120 Days of Sodom and Other Writings / $6.95
B323	SCHUTZ, WILLIAM C. / Joy: Expanding Human Awareness / $1.95
B313	SELBY, HUBERT, JR. / Last Exit to Brooklyn / $1.95
E618	SNOW, EDGAR / Red Star Over China / $4.95
B379	STEINER, CLAUDE / Games Alcoholics Play / $1.95
E703	STOPPARD, TOM / Every Good Boy Deserves Favor and Professional Foul: Two Plays / $3.95
B319	STOPPARD, TOM / Rosencrantz and Guildenstern Are Dead / $1.95
B341	SUZUKI, D. T. / Introduction to Zen Buddhism / $1.95
B395	TRUFFAUT, FRANCOIS / The Story of Adele H. Illus. / $2.45
B365	WARNER, SAMUEL J. / Self Realization and Self Defeat / $2.95
E219	WATTS, ALAN W. / The Spirit of Zen / $2.95

GROVE PRESS, INC., 196 West Houston St., New York, N.Y. 10014

202 -331- 7494